KU-215-581

ALDOUS HUXLEY

The Genius and the Goddess

**TRIAD
GRAFTON BOOKS**

LONDON GLASGOW
TORONTO SYDNEY AUCKLAND

Triad
Grafton Books
8 Grafton Street, London W1X 3LA

Published by Triad Grafton 1982
Reprinted 1984, 1987

Triad Paperbacks Ltd is an imprint of
Chatto, Bodley Head & Jonathan Cape Ltd and
Grafton Books, A Division of the Collins Publishing Group

First published in Great Britain by
Chatto & Windus Ltd 1955

ISBN 0-586-05343-3

Printed and bound in Great Britain by
Collins, Glasgow

Set in Baskerville

Aldous Huxley was born in 1894, the third son of Leonard Huxley (the biographer and editor of the *Cornhill Magazine*) and the grandson of Thomas Henry Huxley. His mother, who died when Aldous was fourteen, was the niece of Matthew Arnold; Sir Julian Huxley was his brother.

In 1916 Aldous Huxley took a first in English at Balliol College, Oxford, despite a condition of near-blindness which had developed while he was at Eton. During 1919 he married Maria Nys, a Belgian, and in the same year he joined *The Athenaeum* under Middleton Murry, Katherine Mansfield's husband. His first book of verse had been published in 1916 and two more followed. Then, in 1920, *Limbo*, a collection of short stories, was published. A year later *Crome Yellow*, Huxley's first novel, appeared and his reputation was firmly established. From the first, the public recognized that the strength of Huxley's writing lay in his combination of dazzling dialogue and surface cynicism (often very funny indeed) with a foundation of great conviction in the emancipating influences he was to exert.

For most of the 1920s Huxley lived in Italy but in the 30s moved to Sanary, near Toulon, where he wrote *Brave New World*. During this decade he was deeply concerned with the Peace Pledge Union but left Europe in 1937 as he believed the Californian climate would help his eyesight, a constant burden. It was in California that he became convinced of the value of mystical experience and he described the effects of some of his experiments in this area in *The Doors of Perception* and *Heaven and Hell*.

Maria Nys Huxley died in 1955 and a year later Aldous married Laura Archera, a concert violinist who had become a practising psychotherapist. They continued to live in California where Aldous Huxley died, in 1963.

By the same author

Novels

Point Counter Point
Crome Yellow
Antic Hay
Those Barren Leaves
Brave New World
Eyeless in Gaza
After Many a Summer
Ape and Essence
Time Must Have a Stop
Island

Short Stories

Limbo
Mortal Coils
Little Mexican
Two or Three Graces
Brief Candles
The Gioconda Smile (Collected
    Short Stories)

Biography

Grey Eminence
The Devils of Loudun

Essays and Belles-Lettres

On the Margin
Along the Road
Proper Studies

Do What You Will
Music at Night & Vulgarity in
    Literature
Texts and Pretexts
    (Anthology)
The Olive Tree
Ends and Means
The Art of Seeing
The Perennial Philosophy
Science, Liberty and Peace
Themes and Variations
The Doors of Perception
Heaven and Hell
Adonis and the Alphabet
Brave New World Revisited
Literature and Science
Collected Essays
The Human Situation
    (ed. Piero Ferrucci)
Moksha

Travel

Jesting Pilate
Beyond the Mexique Bay

Poetry and Drama

Verses and a Comedy
The Gioconda Smile

For Children

The Crows of Pearblossom

'The trouble with fiction,' said John Rivers, 'is that it makes too much sense. Reality never makes sense.'

'Never?' I questioned.

'Maybe from God's point of view,' he conceded. 'Never from ours. Fiction has unity, fiction has style. Facts possess neither. In the raw, existence is always one damned thing after another, and each of the damned things is simultaneously Thurber and Michelangelo, simultaneously Mickey Spillane and Thomas à Kempis. The criterion of reality is its intrinsic irrelevance.' And when I asked, 'To what?' he waved a square brown hand in the direction of the bookshelves. 'To the Best that has been Thought and Said,' he declaimed with mock portentousness. And then, 'Oddly enough, the closest to reality are always the fictions that are supposed to be the least true.' He leaned over and touched the back of a battered copy of *The Brothers Karamazov*. 'It makes so little sense that it's almost real. Which is more than can be said for any of the academic kinds of fiction. Physics and chemistry fiction. History fiction. Philosophy fiction . . .' His accusing finger moved from Dirac to Toynbee, from Sorokin to Carnap. 'More than can be said even for Biography fiction. Here's the latest specimen of the genre.'

From the table beside him he picked up a volume in a glossy blue dust-jacket and held it up for my inspection.

'*The Life of Henry Maartens*,' I read out with no more interest than one accords to a household word. Then I remembered that, to John Rivers, the name had been something more and other than a household word. 'You were his pupil, weren't you?'

Rivers nodded without speaking.

'And this is the official biography?'

'The official fiction,' he amended. 'An unforgettable picture of the Soap Opera scientist – you know the type – the moronic baby with the giant intellect; the sick genius battling indomitably against enormous odds; the lonely thinker who was yet the most affectionate of family men; the absent-minded Professor with his head in the clouds but his heart in the right place. The facts, unfortunately, weren't quite so simple.'

'You mean, the book's innacurate?'

'No, it's all true – so far as it goes. After that, it's all rubbish – or rather it's non-existent. And maybe,' he added, 'maybe it *has* to be non-existent. Maybe the total reality is always too undignified to be recorded, too senseless or too horrible to be left unfictionalized. All the same it's exasperating, if one happens to know the facts, it's even rather insulting, to be fobbed off with Soap Opera.'

'So you're going to set the record straight?' I presumed.

'For the public? Heaven forbid!'

'For me, then. In private.'

'In private,' he repeated. 'After all, why not?' He shrugged his shoulders and smiled. 'A little orgy of reminiscence to celebrate one of your rare visits.'

'Anyone would think you were talking about a dangerous drug.'

'But it *is* a dangerous drug,' he answered. 'One escapes into reminiscence as one escapes into gin or sodium amytal.'

'You forget,' I said, 'I'm a writer, and the Muses are the daughters of Memory.'

'And God,' he added quickly, 'is *not* their brother. God isn't the son of Memory; He's the son of Immediate Experience. You can't worship a spirit in spirit, unless you do it now. Wallowing in the past may be good literature. As wisdom, it's hopeless. Time Regained is Paradise Lost,

6

and Time Lost is Paradise Regained. Let the dead bury their dead. If you want to live at every moment as it presents itself, you've got to die to every other moment. That's the most important thing I learned from Helen.'

The name evoked for me a pale young face framed in the square opening of a bell of dark, almost Egyptian hair – evoked, too, the great golden columns of Baalbek, with the blue sky and the snows of the Lebanon behind them. I was an archaeologist in those days, and Helen's father was my boss. It was at Baalbek that I had proposed to her and been rejected.

'If she'd married me,' I said, 'would *I* have learned it?'

'Helen practised what she always refrained from preaching,' Rivers answered. 'It was difficult not to learn from her.'

'And what about my writing, what about those daughters of Memory?'

'There would have been a way to make the best of both worlds.'

'A compromise?'

'A synthesis, a third position subtending the other two. Actually, of course, you can never make the best of one world, unless in the process you've learned to make the best of the other. Helen even managed to make the best of life while she was dying.'

In my mind's eye Baalbek gave way to the campus of Berkeley, and instead of the noiselessly swinging bell of dark hair there was a coil of grey, instead of a girl's face I saw the thin drawn features of an ageing woman. She must have been ill, I reflected, even then.

'I was in Athens when she died,' I said aloud.

'I remember.' And then, 'I wish you'd been here,' he added. 'For her sake – she was very fond of you. And, of course, for *your* sake too. Dying's an art, and at our age we ought to be learning it. It helps to have seen someone who really knew how. Helen knew how to die because she knew how to live – to live now and here and for the greater glory of God. And that necessarily entails dying too there and then and tomorrow and one's own miserable little self. In the process of living as one ought to live, Helen had been dying by daily instalments. When the final reckoning came, there was practically nothing to pay. Incidentally,' Rivers went on after a little silence, '*I* was pretty close to the final reckoning last spring. In fact, if it weren't for penicillin, I wouldn't be here. Pneumonia, the old man's friend. Now they resuscitate you, so that you can live to enjoy your arteriosclerosis or your cancer of the prostate. So, you see, it's all entirely posthumous. Everybody's dead except me, and I'm living on borrowed time. If I set the record straight, it'll be as a ghost talking about ghosts. And anyhow this is Christmas Eve; so a ghost story is quite in order. Besides, you're a very old friend and even if you *do* put it all in a novel, does it really matter?'

His large lined face lit up with an expression of affectionate irony.

'If it does matter,' I assured him, 'I won't.'

This time he laughed outright.

'The strongest oaths are straw to the fire i' the blood,' he quoted. 'I'd rather entrust my daughters to Casanova than my secrets to a novelist. Literary fires are hotter even than sexual ones. And literary oaths are even strawier than the matrimonial or monastic varieties.'

I tried to protest; but he refused to listen.

'If I still wanted to keep it secret,' he said, 'I wouldn't tell you. But when you *do* publish, please remember the usual footnote. You know – any resemblance to any character living or dead is purely coincidental. But *purely*! And now let's get back to those Maartenses. I've got a picture somewhere.' He hoisted himself out of his chair, walked over to the desk and opened a drawer. 'All of us together – Henry and Katy and the children and me. And by a miracle,' he added, after a moment of rustling among the papers in the drawer, 'it's where it ought to be.'

He handed me the faded enlargement of a snapshot. It showed three adults standing in front of a wooden summer house – a small, thin man with white hair and a beaked nose, a young giant in shirt sleeves and, between them, fair-haired, laughing, broad-shouldered and deep-bosomed, a splendid Valkyrie incongruously dressed in a hobble skirt. At their feet sat two children, a boy of nine or ten, and a pig-tailed elder sister in her early teens.

'How old he looks!' was my first comment. 'Old enough to be his children's grandfather.'

'And infantile enough, at fifty-six, to be Katy's baby boy.'

'Rather a complicated incest.'

'But it worked,' Rivers insisted, 'it worked so well that it had come to be a regular symbiosis. He lived on her. And she was there to be lived on – incarnate maternity.'

I looked again at the photograph.

'What a fascinating mixture of styles! Maartens is pure Gothic. His wife's a Wagnerian heroine. The children are straight out of Mrs Molesworth. And you, you . . .' I looked up at the square, leathery face that confronted me from the other side of the fireplace, then back at the snapshot. 'I'd forgotten what a beauty you used to be. A Roman copy of Praxiteles.'

'Couldn't you make me an original?' he pleaded.

I shook my head.

'Look at the nose,' I said. 'Look at the modelling of the jaw. That isn't Athens; that's Herculaneum. But luckily girls aren't interested in art history. For all practical amorous purposes you were the real thing, the genuine Greek god.'

Rivers made a wry face.

'I may have looked the part,' he said. 'But if you think I could act it . . .' He shook his head. 'No Ledas for me, no Daphnes, no Europas. In those days, remember, I was still the unmitigated product of a deplorable upbringing. A Lutheran minister's son and, after the age of twelve, a widowed mother's only consolation. Yes, her *only* consolation, in spite of the fact that she regarded herself as a devout Christian. Little Johnny took first, second and third place; God was just an Also Ran. And of course the only consolation had no choice but to become the model son, the star pupil, the indefatigable scholarship winner, sweating his way through college and postgraduate school with no spare time for anything more subtle than football or the Glee Club, more enlightening than the Reverend Wigman's weekly sermon.'

'But did the girls allow you to ignore them? With a face like *that*?' I pointed at the curly-headed athlete in the snapshot.

Rivers was silent, then answered with another question.

'Did *your* mother ever tell you that the most wonderful wedding present a man could bring his bride was his virginity?'

'Fortunately not.'

'Well, mine did. And she did it, what's more, on her knees, in the course of an extemporary prayer. She was a great one for extemporary praying,' he added parenthetically. 'Better even than my father had been. The sentences flowed more evenly, the language was more genuinely sham-antique. She could discuss our financial situation or reprimand me for my reluctance to eat tapioca pudding, in the very phrases of the Epistle to the Hebrews. As a piece of linguistic virtuosity, it was quite amazing. Unfortunately I couldn't think of it in those terms. The performer was my mother and the occasion solemn. Everything that was said, while she was talking to God, had to be taken with a religious seriousness. Particularly when it was connected with the great unmentionable subject. At twenty-eight, believe it or not, I still had that wedding present for my hypothetical bride.'

There was a silence.

'My poor John,' I said at last.

He shook his head.

'Actually it was my poor mother. She had it all worked out so perfectly. An instructorship in my old university, then an assistant professorship, then a professorship. There would never be any need for me to leave home. And when I was around forty, she'd arrange a marriage for me with some wonderful Lutheran girl who would love her like her own mother. But for the grace of God, there went John Rivers – down the drain. But the grace of God was forthcoming – with a vengeance, as it turned out. One fine morning, a few weeks after I had my PhD, I had a letter from Henry Maartens. He was at St Louis then, working on atoms. Needed another research assistant, had heard good reports of me from my professor, couldn't offer more than a scandalously small salary – but would I be interested? For a budding physicist it was the opportunity of a lifetime. For my poor mother it was the end of everything. Earnestly, agonizingly, she prayed over it. To her eternal credit, God told her to let me go.

'Ten days later a taxi deposited me on the Maartens' doorstep. I remember standing there in a cold sweat, trying to screw up my courage to ring the bell. Like a delinquent schoolboy who has an appointment with the Headmaster. The first elation over my wonderful good fortune had long since evaporated, and for the last few days at home, and during all the endless hours of the journey, I had been thinking only of my own inadequacy. How long would it take a man like Henry Maartens to see through a man like me? A week? A day? More likely an hour! He'd despise me; I'd be the laughing-stock of the laboratory. And things would be just as bad outside the laboratory. Indeed, they might be even worse. The Maartenses had asked me to be their guest until I could find a place of my own. How extraordinarily kind! But also how fiendishly cruel! In the

11

austerely cultured atmosphere of their home I should reveal myself for what I was – shy, stupid, hopelessly provincial. But meanwhile, the Headmaster was waiting. I gritted my teeth and pushed the button. The door was opened by one of those ancient coloured retainers in an old-fashioned play. You know, the kind that was born before Abolition and has been with Miss Belinda ever since. The performance was on the corny side; but it was a sympathetic part and, though she dearly loved to ham it up, Beulah was not merely a treasure; she was, as I soon discovered, well along the road to sainthood. I explained who I was and, as I talked, she looked me over. I must have seemed satisfactory; for there and then she adopted me as a long-lost member of the family, a kind of Prodigal Son just back from the husks. "I'll go make you a sandwich and a nice cup of coffee," she insisted, and adding, "They're all in here." She opened a door and pushed me through it. I braced myself for the Headmaster and a barrage of culture. But what I actually walked into was something which, if I had seen it fifteen years later, I might have mistaken for a parody, in the minor key, of the Marx Brothers. I was in a large, extremely untidy living-room. On the sofa lay a white-haired man with his shirt collar unbuttoned, apparently dying – for his face was livid, his breath came and went with a kind of wheezing rattle. Close beside him in a rocking-chair – her left hand on his forehead and a copy of William James's *Pluralistic Universe* in her right – the most beautiful woman I had ever seen was quietly reading. On the floor were two children – a small red-headed boy playing with a clockwork train and a girl of fourteen with long black legs, lying on her stomach and writing poetry (I could see the shape of the stanzas) with a red pencil. All were so deeply absorbed in what they were engaged upon – playing or composing, reading or dying – that for at least half a minute my presence in the room remained completely unnoticed. I coughed, got no reaction, coughed again. The small boy raised his head, smiled at me politely but without interest, and returned to his train. I waited another ten seconds; then, in desperation, advanced into the room. The recumbent poetess blocked my path. I stepped over her. "Pardon me," I murmured. She paid no attention; but the reader of William James heard and looked up. Over the top of the *Pluralistic Universe* her eyes were brilliantly blue. "Are you the man about the gas furnace?" she asked. Her face was so radiantly lovely that for a moment I couldn't say a word. I could only shake my head. "Silly!" said the small boy. "The gas man has a moustache." "I'm Rivers," I finally managed to mumble. "Rivers?" she repeated blankly. "Rivers? Oh, *Rivers*!" There was a sudden dawn of recognition. "I'm so glad . . ." But before she could finish the sentence, the man with the death rattle opened a pair of ghastly eyes, made a noise like an indrawn war whoop and, jumping up, rushed toward the open window. "Look out!" the small boy shouted. "Look *out*!" There was a crash. "Oh, Christ!" he added in a tone of contained despair. A whole Grand Central Station lay in ruins, reduced to its component blocks. "Christ!" the child repeated; and when the poetess told him he mustn't say Christ, "I'll say something *really* bad," he menaced. "I'll say . . ." His lips moved in silent blasphemy.

'From the window, meanwhile, came the dreadful sound of a man being slowly hanged.

'"Excuse me," said the beautiful woman. She rose, put down her book and hurried to the rescue. There was a metallic clatter. The hem of her skirt had overturned a signal. The small boy uttered a shriek of rage. "You *fool*," he yelled. "You . . . you *elephant*."

'"Elephants," said the poetess didactically, "always look where they're going." Then she screwed her head round and, for the first time, acknowledged my existence. "They'd forgotten all about you," she explained to me in a

13

tone of wearily contemptuous superiority. "That's how things are around here."

'Over by the window the gradual hanging was still in progress. Doubled up, as though someone had hit him below the belt, the white-haired man was fighting for air – fighting what looked and sounded like a losing battle. Beside him stood the goddess, patting his back and murmuring words of encouragement. I was appalled. This was the most terrible thing I had ever seen. A hand plucked at the cuff of my trousers. I turned and found the poetess looking up at me. She had a narrow, intense little face with grey eyes, set wide apart and a size too large. "*Gloom*," she said. "I need three words to rhyme with *gloom*. I've got *room* – that fits all right. And I've got *womb* – which is simply gorgeous. But what about *catacomb?* . . ." She shook her head; then, frowning at her paper, she read aloud, "*The something gloom Of my soul's deep and dreary catacomb.* I don't like it, do you?" I had to admit that I didn't. "And yet it's exactly what I want to say," she went on. I had a brain wave. "What about *tomb?*" Her face lit up with pleasure and excitement. But of course, of course! What a fool she had been! The red pencil started to scribble at a furious rate. "*The something gloom,*" she declaimed triumphantly, "*Of my soul's irremediable tomb.*" I must have looked dubious, for she hastily asked me if I thought *irrevocable tomb* would be better. Before I could answer there was another, louder sound of strangling. I glanced towards the window, then back at the poetess. "Isn't there anything we can do?" I whispered. The girl shook her head. "I looked it up in the *Encyclopaedia Britannica*," she answered. "It says there that asthma never shortened anybody's life." And then, seeing that I was still disturbed, she shrugged her bony little shoulders and said, "You kind of get used to it."'

Rivers laughed to himself as he savoured the memory. '"You kind of get used to it,"' he repeated. 'Fifty per cent of the Consolations of Philosophy in seven words. And the other fifty per cent can be expressed in six: Brother, when you're dead, you're dead. Or if you prefer, you can make it seven: Brother, when you're dead, you're *not* dead.'

He got up and started to mend the fire.

'Well, that was my first introduction to the Maartens family,' he said as he laid another oak log on the pile of glowing embers. 'I kind of got used to everything pretty quickly. Even to the asthma. It's remarkable how easy it is to get used to other people's asthma. After two or three experiences I was taking Henry's attacks as calmly as the rest of them. One moment he'd be strangling; the next he was as good as new and talking nineteen to the dozen about quantum mechanics. And he continued to repeat the performance till he was eighty-seven. Whereas *I* shall be lucky,' he added, giving the log a final poke, 'if I go to sixty-seven. I was an athlete, you see. One of those strong-as-a-horse boys. And never a day's illness – until, bang, comes a coronary, or whoosh, go the kidneys! Meanwhile the broken reeds, like poor old Henry, go on and on, complaining of ill health until they're a hundred. And not merely complaining – actually suffering. Asthma, dermatitis, every variety of belly-ache, inconceivable fatigues, indescribable depressions. He had a cupboard in his study and another at the laboratory, chock full of little bottles of homoeopathic remedies, and he never stirred out of the house without his Rhus Tox, his Carbo Veg and Bryonia and Kali Phos. His sceptical colleagues used to laugh at him for dosing himself with medicines so prodigiously diluted that, in any given pill, there couldn't be so much as a simple molecule of the curative substance.

'But Henry was ready for them. To justify homoeopathy, he had developed a whole theory of non-material fields – fields of pure energy, fields of unembodied organization. In those days it sounded preposterous. But Henry, don't forget, was a man of genius. Those preposterous notions of his are now beginning to make sense. A few more years, and they'll be self-evident.'

'What *I'm* interested in,' I said, 'is the belly-aches. Did the pills work or didn't they?'

Rivers shrugged his shoulders.

'Henry lived to eighty-seven,' he answered, as he resumed his seat.

'But wouldn't he have lived to eighty-seven without the pills?'

'That,' said Rivers, 'is a perfect example of a meaningless question. We can't revive Henry Maartens and make him live his own life over again without homoeopathy. Therefore, we can never know how his self-medication was related to his longevity. And where there's no possible operational answer, there's no conceivable sense in the question. That's why,' he added, 'there can never be a science of history – because you can never test the truth of any of your hypotheses. Hence the ultimate irrelevance of all these books. And yet you have to read the damned things. Otherwise how can you find your way out of the chaos of immediate fact? Of course it's the wrong way; that goes without saying. But it's better to find even the wrong way than to be totally lost.'

'Not a very reassuring conclusion,' I ventured.

'But the best we can reach – at any rate, in our present condition.' Rivers was silent for a moment. 'Well, as I say,' he resumed in another tone, 'I kind of got used to Henry's asthma, I kind of got used to all of them, to everything. So much so, indeed, that when, after a month of house-hunting, I finally located a cheap and not too nasty apartment, they wouldn't let me go. "Here you are," said Katy, "and here you stay." Old Beulah backed her up. So did Timmy and, though she was of an age and in a mood to dissent from anything anyone else approved of, so, rather grudgingly, did Ruth. Even the great man emerged for a moment from Cloud Cuckoo Land to cast a vote in favour of my staying on. That clinched it. I became a fixture; I became an honorary Maartens. It made me so happy,' Rivers went on after a pause, 'that I kept thinking uneasily that there must surely be something wrong. And pretty soon I saw what it was. Happiness with the Maartenses entailed disloyalty to home. It was an admission that, all the time I lived with my mother, I had never experienced anything but constraint and a chronic sense of guilt. And now, as a member of this family of pagan stangers, I felt not merely happy, but also good; also, in an entirely unprecedented way, religious. For the first time I knew what all those words in the Epistles really meant. *Grace*, for example – I was chock full of grace. *The newness of the spirit* – it was there all the time; whereas most of what I had known with my mother was the deadening oldness of the letter. And what about First Corinthians, thirteen? What about *faith, hope and charity*? Well, I don't want to boast, but I had them. Faith first of all. A redeeming faith in the universe and in my fellow man. As for the other brand of faith – that simple, Lutheran variety which my poor mother was so proud of having preserved intact, like a virginity, through all the temptations of my scientific education . . .' He shrugged his shoulders. 'Nothing can be simpler than zero; and that, I suddenly discovered, was the simple faith I had been living by for the past ten years. At St Louis I had the genuine article – real faith in a real good, and at the same time a hope amounting to the positive conviction that everything would always be wonderful. And along with faith and hope went an overflowing charity. How could you feel affection for someone like Henry – someone so remote that he hardly knew who you were and so self-centred that he didn't even want to know? You couldn't be fond of him – and yet I was, I was. I liked him not merely for the obvious reasons – because he was a great man, because working with him was like having your own intelligence and insight raised to a higher power. I even liked him outside the laboratory, for the very qualities that

17

made it all but impossible to regard him as anything but a kind of high-class monster. I had so much charity in those days that I could have loved a crocodile, I could have loved an octopus. One reads all these fictions of the sociologists, all this learned foolery by the political scientists.' With a gesture of contemptuous exasperation Rivers slapped the backs of a row of corpulent volumes on the seventh shelf. 'But actually there's only one solution, and that's expressible in a four-letter word, so shocking that even the Marquis de Sade was chary of using it.' He spelled it out. 'L-O-V-E. Or if you prefer the decent obscurity of the learned languages, *Agape, Caritas, Mahakaruna*. In those days I really knew what it meant. For the first time – yes, for the first time. That was the only disquieting feature in an otherwise blissful situation. For if this was the first time I knew what loving was, what about all the other times when I had thought I knew, what about those sixteen years of being my mother's only consolation?'

In the ensuing pause I summoned up the memory of the Mrs Rivers who had sometimes come, with her little Johnny, to spend a Sunday afternoon with us on the farm, nearly fifty years ago. It was a memory of black alpaca, of a pale profile like the face on Aunt Esther's cameo brooch, of a smile whose deliberate sweetness didn't seem to match the cool appraising eyes. The picture was associated with a chilling sense of apprehension. 'Give Mrs Rivers a big kiss.' I obeyed, but with what horrified reluctance! A phrase of Aunt Esther's came up, detached, like a single bubble, out of the depths of the past. 'That poor kid,' she had said, 'he just *worships* his mother.' He had worshipped, yes. But had he loved her?

'Is there such a word as "debellishment"?' Rivers suddenly asked.

I shook my head.

'Well, there ought to be,' he insisted. 'For that's what I resorted to in my letters home. I recorded the facts; but I

18

systematically debellished them. I turned a revelation into something drab and ordinary and moralistic. Why was I staying on at the Maartenses? Out of a sense of duty. Because Dr M couldn't drive a car and I was able to help with the fetching and carrying. Because the children had had the misfortune to strike a pair of inadequate teachers and needed all the coaching I could give them. Because Mrs M had been so very kind that I felt I simply *had* to stay and relieve her of a few of her burdens. Naturally I should have preferred my privacy; but would it have been right to put my personal inclinations before their needs? And since the question was addressed to my mother, there could, of course, be only one answer. What hypocrisy, what a pack of lies! But the truth would have been much too painful for her to hear or for me to put into words. For the truth was that I had never been happy, never loved, never felt capable of spontaneous unselfishness until the day I left home and came to live with these Amalekites.'

Rivers sighed and shook his head.

'My poor mother,' he said. 'I suppose I could have been kinder to her. But however kind I might have been, it wouldn't have altered the fundamental facts – the fact that she loved me possessively, and the fact that I didn't want to be possessed; the fact that she was alone and had lost everything, and the fact that I had my new friends; the fact that she was a proud Stoic, living in the illusion that she was a Christian, and the fact that I had lapsed into a wholesome paganism and that, whenever I could forget her – which was every day except Sundays, when I wrote her my weekly letter – I was supremely happy. Yes, supremely happy! For me, in those days, life was an eclogue interspersed with lyrics. Everything was poetry. Driving Henry to the laboratory in my second-hand Maxwell; mowing the lawn; carrying Katy's groceries home in the rain – pure poetry. So was taking Timmy to the station to look at engines. So was taking Ruth for walks in springtime to look for caterpillars. She took a professional interest in caterpillars,' he explained, when I expressed my surprise. 'It was part of the Gloom-Tomb syndrome. Caterpillars were the nearest approach, in real life, to Edgar Allen Poe.'

'To Edgar Allen Poe?'

'"For the play is the tragedy, Man,"' he declaimed, '"and its hero, the Conqueror Worm." In May and June the landscape was fairly crawling with Conqueror Worms.'

'Nowadays,' I reflected, 'it wouldn't be Poe. She'd be reading Spillane or one of the more sadistic comics.'

He nodded his agreement.

'Anything, however bad, provided it has some death in it. Death,' he repeated, 'preferably violent, preferably in the form of guts and corruption – it's one of the appetites of childhood. Almost as strong as the appetite for dolls or candy or playing with the genital organs. Children need death in order to get a new, disgustingly delicious kind of thrill. No, that's not quite accurate. They need it, as they need the other things, in order to give a specific form to the thrills they already have. Can you remember how acute your sensations were, how intensely you felt about everything, when you were a child? The rapture of raspberries and cream, the horror of fish, the hell of castor oil! And the torture of having to get up and recite before the whole class! The inexpressible joy of sitting next to the driver, with the smell of horse sweat and leather in one's nostrils, the white road stretching away to infinity, and the fields of corn and cabbages slowly turning, as the buggy rolled past, slowly opening and shutting like enormous fans. When you're a child, your mind is a kind of saturated solution of feeling, a suspension of all the thrills – but in a latent state, in a condition of indeterminacy. Sometimes it's external circumstances that act as the crystallizing agent, sometimes it's your own imagination. You want some special kind of thrill, and you deliberately work away at yourself until you get it – a bright pink crystal of pleasure, for example, a green or bruise-coloured lump of fear; for fear, of course, is a thrill like any other, fear is a hideous kind of fun. At twelve, I used to enjoy the fun of scaring myself with fantasies about dying, about the hell of my poor father's Lenten sermons. And how much scareder Ruth could get than I could! Scareder at one end of the scale and more rapturously happy at the other. And that's true, I'd say, of most young girls. Their thrill-solution is more concentrated than ours, they can fabricate more kinds of bigger and better crystals more rapidly. Needless to say, I knew nothing about young girls in those days. But Ruth was a liberal education – a bit too liberal, as it turned out later; but we'll come to that in due course. Meanwhile, she had begun to teach me what every young man ought to know about young girls. It was a good preparation for my career as the father of three daughters.'

Rivers drank some whisky and water, put down the glass and for a little while sucked at his pipe in silence.

'There was one particularly educative week-end,' he said at last, smiling to himself at the memory. 'It was during my first spring with the Maartenses. We were staying at their little farmhouse in the country, ten miles west of St Louis. After supper, on the Saturday night, Ruth and I went out to look at the stars. There was a little hill behind the house. You climbed it, and there was the whole sky from horizon to horizon. A hundred and eighty degrees of brute inexplicable mystery. It was a good place for just sitting and saying nothing. But in those days I still felt I had a duty to improve people's minds. So instead of leaving her in peace to look at Jupiter and the Milky Way, I trotted out the stale old facts and figures – the distance in kilometres to the nearest fixed star, the diameter of the galaxy, the latest word from Mount Wilson on the spiral nebulae. Ruth listened, but her mind wasn't improved. Instead, she went into a kind of metaphysical panic. Such spaces, such durations, so many worlds beyond improbable worlds! And here we were, in the face of infinity and eternity, bothering our heads about silence and housekeeping and being on time, about the colour of hair ribbons and the weekly grades in algebra and Latin grammar! Then, in the little wood beyond the hill, an owl began calling, and at once the metaphysical panic turned into something physical – physical but at the same time occult; for this creeping at the pit of the stomach was due to the superstition that owls are wizard birds, bringers of bad luck, harbingers of death. She knew, of course, that it was all nonsense; but how transporting it was to think and act as though it were true! I tried to laugh her out of it; but Ruth wanted to feel scared and was ready to rationalize and justify her fears. "One of the girls in my class's grandmother died last year," she told me. "And that night there was an owl in the garden. Right in the middle of St Louis, where there never are any owls." As if to confirm her story, there was another outburst of distant hooting. The child shuddered and took my arm. We started to walk down the hill in the direction of the wood. "It would absolutely kill me if I was alone," she said. And then, a moment later, "Did you ever read *The Fall of the House of Usher?*" It was evident that she wanted to tell me the story; so I said, No, I hadn't read it. She began. "It's about a brother and sister called Usher, and they lived in a kind of castle with a black and livid tarn in front of it, and there are funguses on the walls, and the brother is called Roderick and he has such a fervid imagination that he can make up poetry without having to think, and he's dark and handsome and has very large eyes and a delicate Hebrew nose, just like his twin sister, who's called Lady Madeline, and they're both very ill with a mysterious nervous complaint and she's liable to go into cataleptic fits . . ." And so the narrative proceeded – a snatch of remembered

Poe, and then a gush of the junior high school dialect of the nineteen-twenties – as we walked down the grassy slope under the stars. And now we were on the road and moving towards the dark wall of woodland. Meanwhile poor Lady Madeline had died and young Mr Usher was roaming about among the tapestries and the fungi in a state of incipient lunacy. And no wonder! "For said I not that my senses were acute?" Ruth declaimed in a thrilling whisper. "I now tell you that I heard her first feeble movements in the hollow coffin. I heard them many, many days ago." Around us the darkness had deepened and suddenly the trees closed over us and we were engulfed in the double night of the wood. Overhead, in the roof of foliage, there was an occasional jagged gleam of a paler, bluer darkness and on either side the tunnel walls opened here and there into mysterious crevices of dim grey crape and blackened silver. And what a mouldy smell of decay! What a damp chill against the cheek! It was as though Poe's fancy had turned into sepulchral fact. We had stepped, so it seemed, into the Ushers' family vault. "And then suddenly," Ruth was saying, "suddenly there was a kind of metallic clang, like when you drop a tray on a stone floor, but sort of muffled, like it was a long way underground, because, you see, there was a huge cellar under the house where all the family was buried. And a minute later there she was at the door – the lofty and enshrouded figure of the Lady Madeline of Usher. And there was blood on her white robes, because she'd been struggling for a whole week to get out of the casket, because of course she'd been buried alive. Lots of people are," Ruth explained. "That's why they advise you to put it in your will – don't bury me until you've touched the soles of my feet with a red-hot iron. If I don't wake up, it's OK and you can go ahead with the funeral. They hadn't done that with the Lady Madeline, and she was just in a cataleptic fit, till she woke up in the coffin. And Roderick had heard her all those days, but for some reason

23

he hadn't said anything about it. And now here she was, all in white, with blood on her, reeling to and fro on the threshold, and then she gave the most frightening shriek and fell on top of him, and he shrieked too and . . ." But at this moment there was a loud commotion in the invisible undergrowth. Black in the blackness, something enormous emerged on to the road just in front of us. Ruth's scream was as loud as Madeline's and Roderick's combined. She clutched my arm, she hid her face against the sleeve. The apparition snorted. Ruth screamed again. There was another snort, then the clatter of retreating hoofs. "It's only a stray horse," I said. But her knees had given way and, if I hadn't caught her and lowered her gently to the ground, she would have fallen. There was a long silence. "When you've had enough of sitting in the dust," I said ironically, "maybe we can go on." "What would you have done if it *had* been a ghost?" she asked at last. "I'd have run away and not come back till it was all over." "What do you mean 'all over'?" she asked. "Well, you know what happens to people who meet ghosts," I answered. "Either they die of fright on the spot, or else their hair turns white and they go mad." But instead of laughing, as I had meant her to do, Ruth said I was a beast and burst into tears. That dark clot, which the horse and Poe and her own fancy had crystallized out of her solution of feeling, was too precious a thing to be lightly parted with. You know those enormous lollipops on sticks that children lick all day long? Well, that's what her fear was – an all-day sucker; and she wanted to make the most of it, to go on sucking and sucking to the deliciously bitter end. It took me the best part of half an hour to get her on her feet again and in her right mind. It was after her bedtime when we got home and Ruth went straight to her room. I was afraid she'd have nightmares. Not at all. She slept like a top and came down to breakfast next morning as gay as a lark. But a lark that had read her Poe, a lark that was still interested in worms. After breakfast we went out caterpillar hunting and found something really stupendous – a big hawk-moth larva, with green and white markings and a horn on its rear end. Ruth poked it with a straw and the poor thing curled itself first one way, then the other, in a paroxysm of impotent rage and fear. "It writhes, it writhes," she chanted exultantly; "with frightful pangs the mimes become its food, and the angels sob at vermin fangs with human blood imbued." But this time the fear-crystal was no bigger than a diamond on a twenty-dollar engagement ring. The thought of death and corruption which she had savoured, the previous night, for the sake of its own intrinsic bitterness, was now a mere condiment, a spice to heighten the taste of life, and make it more intoxicating. "Vermin fangs," she repeated, and gave the green worm another poke, "Vermin fangs . . ." And in an overflow of high spirits she began to sing, "If you were the only girl in the world," at the top of her voice. Incidentally,' Rivers added, 'how significant it is that that disgusting song should crop up as a by-product of every major massacre! It was invented in World War I, revived in World War II and was still being sporadically warbled while the slaughter was going on in Korea. The last word in sentimentality accompanies the last words in Machiavellian power politics and indiscriminate violence. Is that something to be thankful for? Or is it something to deepen one's despair about the human race? I really don't know – do you?'

I shook my head.

'Well, as I was saying,' he resumed, 'she started singing, "If you were the only girl in the world," changed the next line to "and I were the vermin fangs," then broke off, made a dive for Grampus, the cocker spaniel, who eluded her and rushed off, full tilt across the pasture, with Ruth in hot pursuit. I followed at a walk and, when at last I caught up with her, she was standing on a little knoll, with Grampus panting at her feet. The wind was blowing and she was facing into it, like a miniature Victory of Samothrace, the hair lifting from her small flushed face, her short skirt blown back and fluttering like a flag, the cotton of her blouse pressed by the air stream against a thin little body that was still almost as flat and boyish as Timmy's. Her eyes were closed, her lips moved in some silent rhapsody or invocation. The dog turned his head as I approached and wagged a stumpy tail; but Ruth was too far gone into her rapture to hear me. It would have been almost a sacrilege to disturb her; so I halted a few yards away and quietly sat down on the grass. As I watched her, a beatific smile parted her lips and the whole face seemed to glow as though with an inner light. Suddenly her expression changed; she uttered a little cry, opened her eyes and looked about her with an air of frightened bewilderment. "John!" she called thankfully, when she caught sight of me, then ran and dropped on her knees beside me. "I'm so glad you're here," she said. "And there's old Grampus. I almost thought . . ." She broke off and, with the forefinger of her right hand, touched the tip of her nose, her lips, her chin. "Do I look the same?" she asked. "The same," I assured her, "but if anything a little more so." She laughed, and it was a laugh not so much of amusement as of relief. "I was nearly gone," she confided. "Gone where?" I asked. "I don't know," she said, shaking her head. "It was that wind. Blowing and blowing. Blowing everything out of my head – you and Grampus and everyone else, everyone at home, everyone at school, and everything I ever knew or ever cared about. All blown away, and nothing left but the wind and the feeling of my being alive. And they were turning into the same thing and blowing away. And if I'd let go, there wouldn't have been any stopping. I'd have crossed the mountains and gone out over the ocean and maybe right off into one of those black holes between the stars that we were looking at last night." She shuddered. "Do you think I would have died?" she asked. "Or maybe gone into a catalepsy, so that they'd think I was dead, and then I'd have woken up in a coffin." She was back again with Edgar Allen Poe. Next day she showed me a lamentable piece of doggerel, in which the terrors of the night and the ecstasies of the morning had been reduced to the familiar glooms and tombs of all her rhyming. What a gulf between *im*pression and *ex*pression! That's our ironic fate - to have Shakespearean feelings and (unless by some billion-to-one chance we happen to *be* Shakespeare) to talk about them like automobile salesmen, or teenagers, or college professors. We practise alchemy in reverse - touch gold and it turns into lead; touch the pure lyrics of experience, and they turn into the verbal equivalents of tripe and hogwash.'

'Aren't you being unduly optimistic about experience?' I questioned. 'Is it always so golden and poetical?'

'Intrinsically golden,' Rivers insisted. 'Poetical by its essential nature. But of course if you're sufficiently steeped in the tripe and hogwash dished out by the moulders of public opinion, you'll tend automatically to pollute your impressions at the source; you'll re-create the world in the image of your own notions - and of course your own notions are everybody else's notions; so the world you live in will consist of the Lowest Common Denominators of the local culture. But the original poetry is always there - always,' he insisted.

'Even for the old?'

'Yes, even for the old. Provided, of course, that they can recapture their lost innocence.'

'And do you ever succeed, may I ask?'

'Believe it or not,' Rivers answered, 'I sometimes do. Or perhaps it would be truer to say that it sometimes happens to me. It happened yesterday, as a matter of fact, while I was playing with my grandson. From one minute to another - the transformation of lead into gold, of solemn professorial hogwash into poetry, the kind of poetry that life was all the time, while I was with the Maartenses. Every moment of it.'

'Including the moments in the laboratory?'

'Those were some of the best moments,' he answered me. 'Moments of paper work, moments of fiddling around with experimental gadgets, moments of discussion and argument. The whole thing was pure idyllic poetry, like something out of Theocritus or Virgil. Four young PhDs in the rôle of goatherd's apprentices, with Henry as the patriarch, teaching the youngsters the tricks of his trade, dropping pearls of wisdom, spinning interminable yarns about the new pantheon of theoretical physics. He struck the lyre and rhapsodized about the metamorphosis of earth-bound Mass into celestial Energy. He sang the hopeless loves of Electron for her Nucleus. He piped of Quanta and hinted darkly at the mysteries of Indeterminacy. It was idyllic. Those were the days, remember, when you could be a physicist without feeling guilty; the days when it was still possible to believe that you were working for the greater glory of God. Now they won't even allow you the comfort of self-deception. You're paid by the Navy and trailed by the FBI. Not for one moment do they permit you to forget what you're up to. *Ad majorem Dei gloriam?* Don't be an idiot! *Ad majorem hominis degradationem* – that's the thing you're working for. But in 1921 infernal machines were safely in the future. In 1921 we were just a bunch of Theocritan innocents, enjoying the nicest kind of clean scientific fun. And when the fun in the laboratory was over, I'd drive Henry home in the Maxwell and there'd be fun of another kind. Sometimes it was young Timmy, having difficulties with the Rule of Three. Sometimes it was Ruth who simply couldn't see why the square on the hypotenuse must *always* be equal to the sum of the squares on the other two sides. In *this* case, yes; she was ready to admit it. But why *every* time? They would appeal to their father. But Henry had lived so long in the world of Higher Mathematics that he had forgotten how to do sums; and he was interested in Euclid only because

Euclid's was the classical example of reasoning based upon a vicious circle. After a few minutes of utterly confounding talk, the great man would get bored and quietly fade away, leaving me to solve Timmy's problem by some method a little simpler than vector analysis, to set Ruth's doubts at rest by arguments a little less subversive of all faith in rationality than Hillbert's or Poincaré's. And then at supper there would be the noisy fun of the children telling their mother about the day's events at school; the sacrilegious fun of Katy suddenly breaking into a soliloquy on general relativity theory with an accusing question about those flannel pants which Henry was supposed to have picked up at the cleaners; the Old Plantation fun of Beulah's comments on the conversation, or the epic fun of one of her sustained, blow-by-blow accounts of how they used to butcher hogs back on the farm. And later, when the children had gone to bed and Henry had shut himself up in his study there was the fun of funs – there were my evenings with Katy.'

Rivers leaned back in his chair and closed his eyes.

'I'm not much good at visualizing,' he said after a little silence. 'But the wallpaper, I'm pretty sure, was a dusty kind of pink. And the lampshade was certainly red. It must have been red, because there was always that rich flush on her face, as she sat there darning our socks or sewing on the children's buttons. A flush on the face, but never on the hands. The hands moved in the brightness of the unscreened light. What strong hands!' he added, smiling to himself. 'What efficient hands! None of your spiritual, Blessed-Damozellish appendages! Honest to God hands that were good with screwdrivers; hands that could fix things when they went wrong; hands that could give a massage, or when necessary, a spanking; hands that had a genius for pastry and didn't mind emptying slops. And the rest of her matched the hands. Her body – it was the body of a strong young matron. A matron with the face of a

29

healthy, peasant girl. No, that's not quite right. It was the face of a goddess disguised as a healthy peasant girl. Demeter, perhaps. No, Demeter was too sad. And it wasn't Aphrodite either; there was nothing fatal or obsessive about Katy's femininity, nothing self-consciously sexy. If there was a goddess involved, it must have been Hera. Hera playing the part of a milkmaid – but a milkmaid with a mind, a milkmaid who had gone to college.' Rivers opened his eyes and replaced the pipe between his teeth. He was still smiling. 'I remember some of the things she said about the books I used to read aloud in the evenings. H. G. Wells, for example. He reminded her of the rice paddies in her native California. Acres and acres of shiny water, but never more than two inches deep. And those ladies and gentlemen in Henry James's novels – could they ever bring themselves, she wondered, to go to the bathroom? And D. H. Lawrence. How she loved those early books of his! All scientists ought to be compelled to take a post-graduate course in Lawrence. She said that to the Chancellor when he came to dinner. He was a most distinguished chemist; and whether it was *post hoc* or *propter hoc*, I don't know; but his wife looked as if all her secretions were pure acetic acid. Katy's remarks weren't at all well received.' Rivers chuckled. 'And sometimes,' he went on, 'we didn't read; we just talked. Katy told me about her childhood in San Francisco. About the balls and parties after she came out. About the three young men who were in love with her – each one richer and, if possible, stupider than the last. At nineteen she got engaged to the richest and the dumbest. The trousseau was bought, the wedding presents had begun to arrive. And then Henry Maartens came out to Berkeley as a visiting professor. She heard him lecture on the philosophy of science, and after the lecture she went to an evening party given in his honour. They were introduced. He had a nose like an eagle's, he had pale eyes like a Siamese cat's, he looked like the portraits of

Pascal and when he laughed, the noise was like a ton of coke going down a chute. As for what *he* saw – it must have passed description. I knew Katy at thirty-six, when she was Hera. At nineteen she must have been Hebe and the three Graces and all the nymphs of Diana rolled into one. And Henry, remember, had just been divorced by his first wife. Poor woman! she simply wasn't strong enough to play the parts assigned to her – mistress to an indefatigable lover, business manager to an absentee half-wit, secretary to a man of genius, and womb, placenta and circulatory system to the psychological equivalent of a foetus. After two miscarriages and a nervous breakdown she had packed up and gone home to her mother. Henry was on the loose, all four of him – foetus, genius, half-wit and hungry lover – in search of some woman capable of meeting the demands of a symbiotic relationship, in which all the giving would be on her side, all the ravenous and infantile taking on his. The search had been going on for the best part of a year. Henry was growing desperate. And now, suddenly, providentially, here was Katy. It was love at first sight. He took her into a corner and, ignoring everyone else in the room, started to talk to her. Needless to say, it never occurred to him that she might have her own interests and problems, it never entered his head that it might perhaps be a good thing to draw the girl out. He just let fly at her with what happened, for the moment, to be on his mind. On this occasion, it was recent developments in logic. Katy, of course, didn't understand a word of it; but he was so manifestly a genius, it was all so unspeakably wonderful, that there and then, before the evening was over, she made her mother ask him to dinner. He came, he finished off what he had to say and, while Mrs Hanbury and her other guests played bridge he plunged with Katy into semiotics. Three days later there was some sort of a picnic organized by the Audubon Society, and the two of them managed to get separated from the rest of the party in an arroyo. And finally there was the evening when they went to hear *Traviata*. Rum-tum-tum-TUM-te-tum.' Rivers hummed the theme of the prelude to the third act. 'It was irresistible – it always is. On the way home in the cab he kissed her – kissed her with an intensity of passion and at the same time a tact, an adeptness, for which the semiotics and the absent-mindedness had left her entirely unprepared. After that it became only too evident that her engagement to poor dear Randolph had been a mistake. But what a hue and cry, when she announced her intention of becoming Mrs Henry Maartens! A half-mad professor, with nothing but his salary, divorced by his first wife and old enough, into the bargain, to be her father! But all they could say was entirely irrelevant. The only thing that mattered was the fact that Henry belonged to another species; and *that*, not Randolph's – *Homo sapiens* and not *Homo moronicus* – was the species she was now interested in. Three weeks after the earthquake they got married. Had she ever regretted her millionaire? Regretted *Randolph*? To this inconceivably ridiculous question the answer was a peal of laughter. But his horses, she added as she wiped the tears from her eyes, his horses were another matter. His horses were Arabians, and the cattle on his ranch were pure-bred Herefords, and he had a big pond behind the ranch house, with all kinds of the most heavenly ducks and geese. The worst of being a poor professor's wife in a big town was that you never had a chance of getting away from people. Sure, there were plenty of good people, intelligent people. But the soul cannot live by people alone; it needs horses, it needs pigs and waterfowl. Randolph could have provided her with all the animals her heart could desire – but at a price: himself. She had sacrificed the animals and chosen genius – genius with all its drawbacks. And frankly (she admitted it with a laugh, she talked about it with humorous detachment), frankly there *were* drawbacks. In his own way, albeit for entirely different reasons, Henry could be almost as dumb as Randolph himself. An idiot where human relations were concerned, a prize ass in all the practical affairs of life. But what an unboring ass, what a luminous idiot! Henry could be utterly insupportable; but he was always worth it. *Always!* And maybe, she paid me the compliment of adding, maybe when I got married, my wife would feel the same way about me. Insupportable, but worth it.'

'I thought you said she wasn't consciously sexy,' I commented.

'And it's true,' he said. 'You think she was baiting her hook with flattery. She wasn't. She was just stating a fact. I had my points; but I was also unbearable. Twenty years of formal education and a lifetime of my poor mother had produced a real monster.' On the outspread fingers of his left hand he itemized the monster's components. 'I was a learned bumpkin; I was an athlete who couldn't say Bo to a girl; I was a pharisee with a sense of inferiority, I was a prig who secretly envied the people he disapproved of. And yet, in spite of everything, it was worth while to put up with me. I was enormously well meaning.'

'And in this case, I imagine, you did more than mean well. Were you in love with her?' I asked.

There was a little pause; then Rivers slowly nodded.

'Overwhelmingly,' he said.

'But you couldn't say Bo to a girl.'

'This wasn't a girl,' he answered. 'This was Henry's wife. Bo was unthinkable. Besides, I was an honorary Maartens, and that made her my honorary mother. And it wasn't just a question of morality. I never *wanted* to say Bo. I loved her metaphysically, almost theologically – the way Dante loved Beatrice, the way Petrarch loved Laura. With one slight difference, however. In *my* case it happened to be sincere. I actually *lived* my idealism. No little illegitimate Petrarchs on the side. No Mrs Alighieri, and none of those whores that Dante found it necessary to resort to. It was passion, but it was also chastity; and both at white heat.

Passion and chastity,' he repeated, and shook his head. 'At sixty one forgets what the words stand for. Today I only know the meaning of the word that has replaced them – indifference. *Io son Beatrice*,' he declaimed. 'And all is dross that is not Helena. So what? Old age has something else to think about.'

Rivers was silent; and suddenly, as though to elucidate what he had been saying, there was only the ticking of the clock on the mantelpiece, and the whispers of flames among the logs.

'How can anyone seriously believe in his own identity?' he went on. 'In logic, A equals A. Not in fact. Me-now is one kettle of fish; me-then is another. I look at the John Rivers who felt that way about Katy. It's like a puppet play, it's like Romeo and Juliet through the wrong end of the opera glasses. No, it's not even that; it's like looking through the wrong end of the opera glasses at the ghosts of Romeo and Juliet. And Romeo once called himself John Rivers, and was in love, and had at least ten times more life and energy than at ordinary times. And the world he was living in – how totally transfigured!

'I remember how he looked at landscapes; and the colours were incomparably brighter, the patterns that things made in space unbelievably beautiful. I remember how he glanced around him in the streets, and St Louis, believe it or not, was the most splendid city ever built. People, houses, trees, T-model Fords, dogs at lamp-posts – everything was more significant. Significant, you may ask, of what? And the answer is: themselves. These were realities, not symbols. Goethe was absolutely wrong. *Alles vergängliche* is NOT a *Gleichnis*. At every instant every transience is eternally that transience. What it signifies is its own being, and that being (as one sees so clearly when one's in love) is the same as Being with the biggest possible B. Why do you love the woman you're in love with? Because she *is*. And that, after all, is God's own definition of

Himself: I am that I am. The girl is who she is. Some of her isness spills over and impregnates the entire universe. Objects and events cease to be the mere representatives of classes and become their own uniqueness; cease to be illustrations of verbal abstractions and become fully concrete. Then you stop being in love, and the universe collapses, with an almost audible squeak of derision, into its normal insignificance. Could it ever *stay* transfigured? Maybe it could. Maybe it's just a question of being in love with God. But that,' Rivers added, 'is neither here nor there. Or rather it's the only thing that's either here, there or anywhere; but if we said so, we'd be cut by all our respectable friends and might even end up in the asylum. So let's get back as quickly as possible to something a little less dangerous. Back to Katy, back to the late lamented . . .'

He broke off.

'Did you hear something?'

This time I distinctly did. It was the sound, muffled by distance and a heroic self-restraint, of a child's sobbing.

Rivers got up and, thrusting his pipe into his pocket, walked to the door and opened it.

'Bimbo?' he called questioningly, and then to himself: 'How the devil did he get out of his crib?'

For all answer there was a louder sob.

He moved out into the hall and a moment later there was the sound of heavy footsteps on the stairs.

'Bimbo,' I heard him say, 'good old Bimbo! Come to see if you could catch Santa Claus red-handed – was that it?'

The sobbing mounted to a tragic crescendo. I got up and followed my host upstairs. Rivers was sitting on the top step, his arms, gigantic in their rough tweed, around a tiny figure in blue pyjamas.

'It's grandpa,' he kept repeating. 'Funny old grandpa. Bimbo's all right with grandpa.' The sobbing gradually died down. 'What made Bimbo wake up?' Rivers asked.

'What made him climb out of his crib?'

'Dog,' said the child, and at the memory of his dream he began to cry again. 'Big dog.'

'Dogs are funny,' Rivers assured him. 'Dogs are so dumb they can't say anything but bow-wow. Think of all the things Bimbo can say. Mummy. Weewee. Daddy. Pussycat. Dogs aren't smart. They can't say any of those things. Just bow-wow-wow.' He put on an imitation of a bloodhound. 'Or else bow-wow-wow.' This time it was a toy Pomeranian. 'Or else Wo-o-o-ow.' He howled lugubriously and grotesquely. Uncertainly, between sobs, the child began to laugh. 'That's right,' said Rivers. 'Bimbo just laughs at those dumb dogs. Every time he sees one, every time he hears that silly barking, he laughs and laughs and laughs.' This time the child laughed whole-heartedly. 'And now,' said Rivers, 'grandpa and Bimbo are going to take a walk.' Still holding the child in his arms, he got up and made his way along the corridor. 'This is grandpa's room,' he said, opening the first door. 'Nothing of great interest here, I'm afraid.' The next door stood ajar; he walked in. 'And this is Mummy's and Daddy's room. And here's the closet with all Mummy's clothes. Don't they smell good?' He sniffed loudly. The child followed suit. '*Le Shocking de Schiaparelli*,' Rivers went on. 'Or is it *Femme*? Anyhow, it serves the same purpose; for it's sex, sex, sex that makes the world go round – as, I'm sorry to say, you'll find out, my poor Bimbo, in a very few years from now.' Tenderly he brushed his cheek against the pale floss of the child's hair, then walked over to the full length mirror set in the door of the bathroom. 'Look at us,' he called to me. 'Just look at us!'

I came and stood beside him. There we were in the glass – a pair of bent and sagging elders and, in the arms of one of them, a small, exquisite Christ-child.

'And to think,' said Rivers, 'to think that once we were all like that. You start as a lump of protoplasm, a machine for eating and excreting. You grow into this sort of thing. Something almost supernaturally pure and beautiful.' He laid his cheek once more against the child's head. 'Then comes a bad time with pimples and puberty. After which you have a year or two, in your twenties, of being Praxiteles. But Praxiteles soon puts on weight and starts to lose his hair and for the next forty years you degenerate into one or other of the varieties of the human gorilla. The spindly gorilla – that's you. Or the leather-faced variety – that's me. Or else it's the successful business-man type of gorilla – you know, the kind that looks like a baby's bottom with false teeth. As for the female gorillas, the poor old things with paint on their cheeks and orchids at the prow . . . No, let's not talk about them, let's not even think.'

The child in his arms yawned at our reflections, then turned, pillowed his head on the man's shoulder and closed his eyes. 'I think we can take him back to his crib,' Rivers whispered and started towards the door.

'One feels,' he said slowly, as we stood looking down, a few minutes later, at that small face, which sleep had transfigured into the image of an unearthly serenity, 'one feels so desperately sorry for them. They don't know what they're in for. Seventy years of ambushes and betrayals, of booby traps and deceptions.'

'*And* of fun,' I put in. 'Fun to the pitch, sometimes, of ecstasy.'

'Of course,' Rivers agreed, as he turned away from the crib. 'That's what baits the booby traps.' He switched off the light, softly closed the door and followed me down the stairs. 'Fun – every kind of fun. Sex fun, eating fun, power fun, comfort fun, possession fun, cruelty fun. But there's either a hook in the bait, or else when you grab it, it pulls a trigger and down come the bricks or the bucket of bird lime or whatever it is that the cosmic joker has prepared for you.' We resumed our seats on either side of the fire in the

37

library. 'What sort of traps are waiting for that poor little shining creature up there in the crib? One can hardly bear to think of it. The only comfort is that there's ignorance before the event and, after it, forgetting, or at the very least indifference. Every balcony scene turns into an affair of midgets in another universe! And in the end, of course, there's always death. And while there is death, there is hope.' He refilled our glasses and relit his pipe. 'Where was I?'

'In heaven,' I answered, 'with Mrs Maartens.'

'In heaven,' Rivers repeated. And then, after a little pause, 'It lasted,' he went on, 'about fifteen months. From December to the second spring, with a break of ten weeks in the summer, while the family was away in Maine. Ten weeks of what was supposed to be my vacation at home, but was actually, in spite of the familiar house, in spite of my poor mother, the most desolate kind of exile. And it wasn't only Katy that I missed. I was homesick for all of them – for Beulah in the kitchen, for Timmy on the floor with his trains, for Ruth and her preposterous poems, for Henry's asthma and the laboratory and those extraordinary monologues of his about everything. What bliss it was, in September, to regain my paradise! Eden in autumn, with the leaves turning, the sky still blue, the light changing from gold to silver. Then Eden in winter, Eden with the lamps lighted and rain outside the windows, the bare trees like hieroglyphs against the sunset. And then, at the beginning of that second spring, there was a telegram from Chicago. Katy's mother was ill. Nephritis – and those were the days before the sulfas, before penicillin. Katy packed her bags and was at the station in time to catch the next train. The two children – the three children, if you counted Henry – were left in charge of Beulah and myself. Timmy gave us no trouble at all. But the others, I assure you, the others more than made up for Timmy's reasonableness. The poetess refused to eat her prunes at breakfast, couldn't be bothered to brush her hair, neglected her homework. The Nobel Prize winner wouldn't get up in the morning, cut his lectures, was late for every appointment. And there were other, graver delinquencies. Ruth broke her piggy bank and squandered a year's accumulated savings on a make-up kit and a bottle of cheap perfume. The day after Katy left, she looked and smelt like the Whore of Babylon.'

'For the benefit of the Conqueror Worm?'

'Worms were out,' he answered. 'Poe was as old-fashioned as *Over There* or *Alexander's Ragtime Band*. She'd been reading Swinburne, she'd just made the discovery of the poems of Oscar Wilde. The universe was quite different now and she herself was somebody else – another poetess with a brand new vocabulary . . . Sweet sin; jasper claws; the ache of purple pulses; the raptures and roses of vice; and lips, of course, lips inter-twisted and bitten till the foam has a savour of blood – all that adolescent bad taste of Late-Victorian rebellion. And in Ruth's case, the new words had been accompanied by new facts. She was no longer a little boy in a skirt and with pigtails; she was a budding woman with two little breasts that she carried about delicately and gingerly as though they were a pair of extremely valuable but rather dangerous and embarrassing zoological specimens. They were a source, one could sense, of mingled pride and shame, of intense pleasure and, therefore, of a haunting sense of guilt. How impossibly crude our language is! If you don't mention the physiological correlates of emotion, you're being false to the given facts. But if you do mention them, it sounds as though you were trying to be gross and cynical. Whether it's passion or the desire of the moth for the star, whether it's tenderness or adoration or romantic yearning – love is always accompanied by events in the nerve endings, the skin, the mucous membranes, the glandular and erectile tissues. Those who don't say so are liars. Those who do are labelled as pornographers. It's the fault, of course, of our philosophy of life; and our philosophy of life is the inevitable by-product of a language that separates in idea what in actual fact is always inseparable. It separates and at the same time it evaluates. One of the abstractions is "good", and the other is "bad". *Judge not that ye be not judged.* But the nature of language is such that we can't help judging. What we need is another set of words. Words that can express the natural togetherness of things. Muco-spiritual, for example, or dermatocharity. Or why not mastonoetic? Why not viscerosophy? But translated, of course, out of the indecent obscurity of a learned language into something you could use in everyday speech or even in lyrical poetry. How hard it is, without those still non-existent words, to discuss even so simple and obvious a case as Ruth's! The best one can do is to flounder about in metaphors. A saturated solution of feelings, which can be crystallized either from the outside or the inside. Words and events that fall into the psycho-physical soup and make it clot into action-producing lumps of emotion and sentiment. Then come the glandular changes, and the appearance of those charming little zoological specimens which the child carries around with so much pride and embarrassment. The thrill-solution is enriched by a new kind of sensibility that radiates from the nipples, through the skin and the nerve-ends, into the soul, the subconscious, the superconscious, the spirit. And these new psycho-erectile elements of personality impart a kind of motion to the thrill-solution, cause it to flow in a specific direction – towards the still unmapped, undifferentiated region of love. Into this flowing stream of love-oriented feeling chance drops a variety of crystallizing agents – words, events, other people's example, private phantasies and memories, all the innumerable devices used by the Fates to mould an individual human destiny. Ruth had the misfortune to pass from Poe to Algernon and Oscar, from

40

the *Conqueror Worm* to *Dolores* and *Salome*. Combined with the new facts of her own physiology, the new literature made it absolutely necessary for the poor child to smear her mouth with lipstick and drench her combinations with synthetic violet. And worse was to follow.'

'Synthetic ambergris?'

'Much worse – synthetic love. She persuaded herself that she was passionately Swinburneishly in love – and, of all people, with *me*!'

'Couldn't she have chosen someone a little nearer her own size?' I asked.

'She'd tried,' Rivers answered, 'but it hadn't worked. I had the story from Beulah, to whom she had confided it. A tragic little story of a fifteen-year-old girl adoring a heroic young footballer and scholarship-winner of seventeen. She had chosen someone more nearly her own size; but unfortunately, at that period of life, two years are an almost impassable gulf. The young hero was interested only in girls of a muturity comparable to his own – eighteen-year-olds, seventeen-year-olds, at a pinch well-developed sixteen-year-olds. A skinny little fifteen-year-old like Ruth was out of the question. She found herself in the position of a low-born Victorian maiden hopelessly adoring a duke. For a long time the young hero didn't even notice her; and when at last she forced herself on his attention, he began by being amused and ended up by being rude. That was when she started to persuade herself that she was in love with me.'

'But if seventeen was too old, why did she try twenty-eight? Why not sixteen?'

'There were several reasons. The rebuff had been public, and if she'd chosen some pimply younger substitute for the footballer, the other girls would have commiserated with her to her face and laughed at her behind her back. Love for another schoolboy was thus out of the question. But she knew no males except schoolboys and myself. There was no

41

choice. If she was going to love anybody – and the new physiological facts inclined her to love, the new vocabulary imposed love upon her as a categorical imperative – then I was the man. It started actually several weeks before Katy left for Chicago. I had noticed a number of premonitory symptoms – blushings, silences, abrupt inexplicable exits in the middle of conversations, fits of jealous sulking if ever I seemed to prefer the mother's company to the child's. And then, of course, there were those love poems which she insisted, in the teeth of her own and my embarrassment, on showing me. *Blisses and kisses. Lips and whips, yearning and burning. Best, blest, pressed, breast.* She'd look at me intently while I read the things, and it wasn't the merely anxious look of a literary novice awaiting the critic's judgment; it was the damp, large, lustrous regard of an adoring spaniel, of a Counter-Reformation Magdalen, of the willing murderee at the feet of her predestined Bluebeard. It made me feel exceedingly uncomfortable, and I wondered sometimes if it wouldn't be a good thing, for everybody's sake, to mention the matter to Katy. But then, I argued, if my suspicions were unfounded, I should look pretty fatuous; and if I were right, I should be making trouble for poor little Ruth. Better say nothing and wait for the foolishness to blow over. Better to go on pretending that the poems were simply literary exercises which had nothing to do with real life or the author's feelings. And so it went on, underground, like a Resistance Movement, like the Fifth Column, until the day of her mother's departure. Driving home from the station I wondered apprehensively what would happen now that Katy's restraining presence had been removed. Next morning brought the answer – painted cheeks, a mouth like an over-ripe strawberry and that perfume, that whore-house smell of her!'

'With behaviour, I suppose, to match?'

'That was what I expected, of course. But oddly enough it didn't immediately materialize. Ruth didn't seem to feel the need of *acting* her new part; it was enough merely to *look* it. She was satisfied with the signs and emblems of the grand passion. Scenting her cotton underclothes, looking at the image in the glass of the preposterously raddled little face, she could see and smell herself as another Lola Montez, without having to establish her claim to the title by doing anything at all. And it was not merely the mirror that told her who she had become; it was also public opinion – her amazed and envious and derisive school fellows, her scandalized teachers. Their looks and comments corroborated her private phantasies. She was not the only one to know it; even other people recognized the fact that she had now become the *grande amoureuse*, the *femme fatale*. It was all so novel and exciting and absorbing that for a time, thank heaven, I was almost forgotten. Besides, I had committed the unpardonable offence of not taking her latest impersonation with proper seriousness. It was on the very first day of the new dispensation. I came downstairs to find Ruth and Beulah in the hall, hotly disputing. "A nice young girl like you," the old woman was saying. "You ought to be ashamed of yourself." The nice young girl tried to enlist me as an ally. "You don't think mother will mind my using make-up, do you?" Beulah left me no time to answer. "I'll tell you what your mother will do," she said emphatically and with remorseless realism, "she'll give you one look, then she'll sit down on the davenport, turn you over her knee, pull down your drawers and give you the biggest spanking you ever had in all your life." Ruth gave her a look of cold and haughty contempt and said, "I wasn't talking to you." Then she turned back in my direction. "What do *you* say, John?" The strawberry lips wreathed themselves into what was intended to be a richly voluptuous smile, the eyes gave me a bolder version of their adoring look. "What do *you* say?" In mere self-defence I told her the truth. "I'm afraid Beulah's right," I said. "An enormous spanking." The smile faded, the eyes darkened and narrowed, an angry flush appeared beneath the rouge on her cheeks. "I think you're absolutely disgusting," she said. "Disgusting!" Beulah echoed. "Who's disgusting, I'd like to know?" Ruth scowled and bit her lip, but managed to ignore her. "How old was Juliet?" she asked with a note of anticipated triumph in her voice. "A year younger than you are," I answered. The triumph broke through in a mocking smile. "But Juliet," I went on, "didn't go to school. No classes, no homework. Nothing to think about except Romeo and painting her face – if she *did* paint it, which I rather doubt. Whereas you've got algebra, you've got Latin and the French irregular verbs. You've been given the inestimable opportunity of some day becoming a reasonably civilized young woman." There was a long silence. Then she said, "I hate you." It was the cry of an outraged Salome, of Dolores justly indignant at having been mistaken for a high school kid. Tears began to flow. Charged with the black silt of mascara, they cut their way through the alluvial plains of rouge and powder. "Damn you," she sobbed, "*damn* you!" She wiped her eyes; then, catching sight of the horrible mess on her handkerchief, she uttered a cry of horror and rushed upstairs. Five minutes later, serene and completely repainted, she was on her way to school. And *that*,' Rivers concluded, 'was one of the reasons why our *grande amoureuse* paid so little attention to the object of her devouring passion, why the *femme fatale* preferred, during the first two weeks of her existence, to concentrate on herself rather than on the person to whom the author of the scenario had assigned the part of victim. She had tried me out and found me sadly unworthy of the rôle. It seemed better, for the time being, to play the piece as a monologue. In *that* quarter at least I was given a respite. But meanwhile my Nobel Prize winner was getting into trouble.

'On the fourth day of his emancipation, Henry sneaked off to a cocktail party given by a female musicologist with

Bohemian tastes. Broken reeds can never hold their liquor like gentlemen. Henry could get gloriously tipsy on tea and conversation. Martinis turned him into a maniac, who suddenly became a depressive and ended up, invariably, by vomiting. He knew it, of course, but the child in him had to assert its independence. Katy had confined him to an occasional sherry. Well, he'd show her, he'd prove that he could affront Prohibition as manfully as anyone else. When the cat's away, the mice will play. And they'll play (such is the curious perversity of the human heart) at games which are simultaneously dangerous and boring – games where, if you lose and retire, you feel humiliated and, if you persist and win, you wish to God you hadn't. Henry accepted the musicologist's invitation, and what was bound to happen duly happened. By the time he was halfway through his second drink he was making an exhibition of himself. By the end of the third he was holding the musicologist's hand and telling her that he was the unhappiest man in the world. And a quarter of the way through the fourth he had to make a dash for the bathroom. But that wasn't all; on the way home – he insisted on walking – he managed somehow to lose his briefcase. In it were the first three chapters of his new book. *From Boole to Wittgenstein.* Even now, a generation later, it's still the best introduction to modern logic. A little masterpiece! And maybe it would be still better if he hadn't got drunk and lost the original version of the first three chapters. I deplored the loss, but welcomed its sobering effect on poor old Henry. For the next few days he was as good as gold, as reasonable, very nearly, as little Timmy. I thought my troubles were over, all the more so as the news from Chicago seemed to indicate that Katy would soon be home again. Her mother, so it seemed, was sinking. Sinking so fast that, one morning on our way to the laboratory, Henry made me stop at a haberdasher's; he wanted to buy himself a black satin tie for the funeral.

Then, electrifyingly, came the news of a miracle. At the last moment, refusing to give up hope, Katy had called in another doctor – a young man just out of John Hopkins, brilliant, indefatigable, up to all the latest tricks. He had started a new treatment, he had wrestled with death through the whole of a night and a day and another night. And now the battle was won; the patient had been brought back from the very brink of the grave and would live. Katy, in her letter, was exultant and I, of course, exulted in sympathy. Old Beulah went about her work loudly praising the Lord, and even the children took time off their themes and problems, their phantasies of sex and railway trains, to rejoice. Everyone was happy except Henry. True, he kept saying that he was happy; but his unsmiling face (he could never conceal what he really felt) belied his words. He had been counting on Mrs Hanbury's death to bring his womb-secretary, his mother-mistress home again. And now – unexpectedly, improperly (there was no other word for it) – this interfering young squirt from Johns Hopkins had come along with his damned miracle. Someone who ought to have quietly shuffled off, was now (against all the rules) out of danger. Out of danger; but still, of course, much too sick to be left alone. Katy would have to stay on in Chicago until the patient could fend for herself. Heaven only knew when the one being on whom poor old Henry depended for everything – his health, his sanity, his very life – would return to him. Hope deferred brought on several attacks of asthma. But then, providentially, came the announcement that he had been elected a Corresponding Member of the French Institute. Very flattering, indeed! It cured him instantly – but, alas, not permanently. A week passed, and as day succeeded day, Henry's sense of deprivation became a positive agony, like the withdrawal pains of a drug addict. His anguish found expression in a wild, irrational resentment. That fiendish old hag! (Actually, Katy's mothers was two months his junior.) That malignant malingerer! For, of course, she wasn't *really* ill – nobody could be really ill that long without dying. She was just shamming. And the motive was a mixture of selfishness and spite. She wanted to keep her daughter to herself and she wanted (for the old bitch had always hated him) to prevent Katy from being where she ought to be – with her husband. I gave him a little talk about nephritis and made him re-read Katy's letters. It worked for a day or two, and after that the news was more encouraging. The patient was making such good progress that in a few days, maybe, she could safely be left in charge of a nurse and the Swedish maid. In his joy, Henry became, for the first time since I had known him, almost a normal father. Instead of retiring to his study after dinner, he played games with the children. Instead of talking about his own subjects, he tried to amuse them by making bad puns and asking riddles. "Why is a chicken with its head hanging down like next week?" Obviously, because its neck's weak. Timmy was in ecstasies and even Ruth condescended to smile. Three more days passed and it was Sunday. In the evening we played bezique and then a game of Heads, Bodies and Tails. The clock struck nine. One last round; then the children went upstairs. Ten minutes later they were in bed and calling us to come and say good night. We looked in first on Tommy. "Do you know this one?" Henry asked. "What flower would come up if you planted bags of anger?" The answer, of course, was sacks of rage; but as Timmy had never heard of saxifrage, it left him rather cold. We turned out the light and moved on to the next room. Ruth was in bed with the Teddy Bear, who was at once her baby and her Prince Charming, beside her. She was wearing pale blue pyjamas and full make up. Her teacher had raised objections to rouge and perfume in class and, when persuasion proved unavailing, the Principal had categorically forbidden them. The poetess had been reduced to painting and

47

scenting herself at bedtime. The whole room reeked of imitation violets and the pillow, on either side of her small face, was streaked with lipstick and mascara. These were details, however, which Henry was not the man to notice. "What flower," he asked as he approached the bed, "or, to be more precise, what flowering tree would come up, if you were to plant a packet of old love letters?" "Love letters?" the child repeated. She glanced at me, then blushed and looked away. Forcing a laugh, she answered, in a bored superior tone, that she couldn't guess. "Laburnum," her father brought out triumphantly; and when she didn't understand, "La, burn 'em," he explained. "Don't you get the point? They're love letters – *old* love letters, and you've found a new admirer. So what do you do? You burn them." "But why La?" Ruth asked. Henry gave her a brief, instructive lecture on the art of innocuous blasphemy. Gee for God, Jeeze for Jesus, Heck for Hell, La for Lord. "But nobody ever says La," Ruth objected. "They did in the eighteenth century," Henry retorted rather testily. Far off in the master bedroom, the telephone bell started to ring. His face brightened. "I have a hunch it's Chicago calling," he said, as he bent down to give Ruth her good-night kiss. "And another hunch," he added as he hurried towards the door, "that mother will be coming back tomorrow. Tomorrow!" he repeated, and was gone. "Won't it be wonderful," I said fervently, "if he's right!" Ruth nodded her head and said, "Yes," in a tone that made it sound like "No." The narrow painted face suddenly took on an expression of acute anxiety. She was thinking, no doubt, of what Beulah had said would happen when her mother came home; was seeing, was actually feeling, Dolores-Salome turned over a large maternal knee and, in spite of her being a year older than Juliet, getting resoundingly spanked. "Well, I'd better be going," I said at last. Ruth caught my hand and held it. "Not yet," she pleaded and, as she spoke, her face changed its expression.

48

The pinched anxious look was replaced by a tremulous smile of adoration; the lips parted, the eyes widened and shone. It was as though she had suddenly remembered who I was – her slave and her predestined Bluebeard, the only reason for her assumption of the double rôle of fatal temptress and sacrificial victim. And tomorrow, if her mother came home, tomorrow it would be too late; the play would be over, the theatre closed by order of the police. It was now or never. She squeezed my hand. "Do you like me, John?" she whispered inaudibly. I answered in the jolly, ringing tones of an extraverted scoutmaster, "Of course I like you." "As much as you like mother?" she insisted. I parried with a display of good-humoured impatience. "What an asinine question!" I said. "I like your mother the way one likes grown-ups. And I like you the way . . ." "The way one likes children," she concluded bitterly. "As if *that* made any difference!" "Well, doesn't it?" "Not to *this* kind of thing." And when I asked her what kind of thing, she squeezed my hand and said, "Liking people," and gave me another of those looks of hers. There was an embarrassing pause. "Well, I guess I'd better be going," I said at last, and remembering the rhyme which Timmy always found so exquisitely humorous, "Good night," I added as I disengaged my hand, "sleep tight, mind the fleas don't bite." The joke fell like a ton of pig iron into the silence. Unsmiling, with a focused intensity of yearning that I would have found comic if it hadn't scared me out of my wits, she went on gazing up at me. "Aren't you going to say good night to me properly?" she asked. I bent down to administer the ritual peck on the forehead, and suddenly her arms were around my neck and it was no longer I who was kissing the child, but the child who was kissing me – on the right cheekbone first of all and then, with somewhat better aim, near the corner of the mouth. "Ruth!" I protested; but before I could say more, she had kissed me again, with a clumsy kind of violence, full on the lips. I jerked myself free. "What did you do that for?" I asked in an angry panic. Her face flushed, her eyes shining and enormous, she looked at me, whispered, "I love you," then turned away and buried her face in the pillow next to the Teddy Bear. "All right," I said severely. "This is the last time I come and say good night to you," and I turned to go. The bed creaked, bare feet thudded on the floor and as I touched the door knob she was beside me, tugging at my arm. "I'm sorry, John," she was saying incoherently. "I'm sorry. I'll do anything you say. Anything . . ." The eyes were all spaniel now, without a trace of the temptress. I ordered her back to bed and told her that, if she was a very good girl, I might relent. Otherwise . . . And with that unspoken threat I left her. First I went to my room, to wash the lipstick off my face, then walked back along the corridor towards the stairs and ultimately the library. On the landing at the head of the staircase I almost collided with Henry, as he came out of the passage leading to his wing of the house. "What news?" I began. But then I saw his face and was appalled. Five minutes before he had been gaily asking riddles. Now he was an old, old man, pale as a corpse, but without the corpse's serenity; for there was an expression in his eyes and around the mouth of unbearable suffering. "Is something wrong?" I asked anxiously. He shook his head without speaking. "You're sure?" I insisted. "That was Katy on the phone," he said at last in a toneless voice. "She isn't coming home." I asked if the old lady was worse again. "That's the excuse," he said bitterly, then turned and walked back in the direction from which he had come. Full of concern, I followed him. There was a short passage, I remember, with the door of a bathroom at the end of it and another door on the left, opening into the master bedroom. I had never been in the room before, and it was with a shock of surprise and wonder that I now found myself confronted by the Maartenses' extraordinary bed. It was an Early-American four-poster, but of such gigantic

50

proportions that it made me think of presidential assassinations and state funerals. In Henry's mind, of course, the association of ideas must have been somewhat different. My catafalque was his marriage bed. The telephone, which had just condemned him to another term of solitude, stood next to the symbol and scene of his conjugal happiness. No, that's the wrong word,' Rivers added parenthetically. '"Conjugal" implies a reciprocal relationship between two full-blown persons. But for Henry, Katy wasn't a person; she was his food, she was a vital organ of his own body. When she was absent, he was like a cow deprived of grass, like a man with jaundice struggling to exist without a liver. It was an agony. "Maybe you'd better lie down for a while," I said in the wheedling tone one automatically adopts when speaking to the sick. I made a gesture in the direction of the bed. His response, this time, was like what happens if you sneeze while traversing a slope of newly fallen snow – an avalanche. And what an avalanche! Not the white virginal variety, but a hot, palpitating dung-slide. It stank, it suffocated, it overwhelmed. From the fool's paradise of my belated and utterly inexcusable innocence, I listened in shocked, astonished horror. "It's obvious," he kept repeating. "It's only too obvious." Obvious that if Katy didn't come home, it was because she didn't want to come home. Obvious that she must have found some other man. And obvious that this other man was the new doctor. Doctors were notoriously good lovers. They understood physiology, they knew all about the autonomic nervous system.

'Horror gave place in my mind to indignation. What was he daring to say about my Katy, about this more than woman who could only be as pure and perfect as my own almost religious passion? "Are you seriously implying," I began . . . But Henry wasn't implying. He was categorically affirming. Katy was being unfaithful to him with the young squirt from Johns Hopkins.

51

'I told him he was mad, and he retorted that I knew nothing about sex. Which, of course, was painfully true. I tried to change the subject. It wasn't a question of sex – it was a question of nephritis, of a mother who needed her daughter's care. But Henry wouldn't listen. All he now wanted was to torture himself. And if you ask why he wanted to torture himself, I can only answer that it was because he was already in agony. His was the weaker, the more dependent half of a symbiotic partnership which (so he believed) had just been dissolved abruptly. It was a surgical operation, without anaesthetics. Katy's return would have stopped the pain and instantly healed the wound. But Katy was not returning. *Therefore* (admire the logic!) it was necessary for Henry to inflict upon himself as much additional suffering as he possibly could. And the most effective way of doing that was to put his misery into lacerating words. To talk and talk – not, of course, to me, not even at me; only to himself – but to himself (and this was essential if he was to suffer) in my presence. The part assigned to me was not that of the supporting character actor, not even that of the bit player who serves as confidante and errand-runner. No, I was merely the nameless, almost faceless extra, whose business it had been to provide the hero with his initial excuse for thinking out loud, and who now, by simply being on the spot, imparted to the overheard soliloquy a monstrousness, a sheer obscenity, which it would have lacked if the speaker had been alone. Self-activated, the dung-slide gathered momentum. From Katy's betrayal, he passed to her choice (and this was the unkindest cut) of a younger man. Younger and therefore more virile, more indefatigably lustful. (Not to mention that, as a doctor, he knew about physiology and the autonomic nervous system.) The person, the professional, the devoted healer – all had disappeared; and so, by implication had Katy. Nothing remained except a pair of sexual functions frantically exploiting one another in the void. That he could have thought in these terms about Katy and her hypothetical lover was a proof, as I began obscurely to realize, that he thought in the same way about Katy and himself. Henry, as I've said, was a broken reed, and broken reeds, as you must have had innumerable occasions to observe, are apt to be ardent. Ardent, indeed, to the point of frenzy. No, that's the wrong word. Frenzy is blind. Whereas lovers like Henry never lose their head. They take it with them, however far they go – take it with them so that they can be fully, gloatingly conscious of their own and their partner's alienation. Actually, this was about the only thing, outside his laboratory and his library, that Henry cared to be conscious of. Most people inhabit a universe that is like French *café au lait* – fifty per cent skim milk and fifty per cent stale chicory, half psycho-physical reality and half conventional verbiage. Henry's universe was modelled on the highball. It was a mixture in which half a pint of the fizziest philosophical and scientific ideas all but drowned a small jigger of immediate experience, most of it strictly sexual. Broken reeds are seldom good mixers. They're far too busy with their ideas, their sensuality and their psychosomatic complaints to be able to take an interest in other people – even their own wives and children. They live in a state of the most profound voluntary ignorance, not knowing anything about anybody, but abounding in preconceived opinions about everything. Take the education of children, for example. Henry could talk about it as an authority. He had read Piaget, he had read Dewey, he had read Montessori, he had read the psycho-analysts. It was all there in his cerebral filing cabinet, classified, categorized, instantly available. But when it came to doing something for Ruth and Timmy, he was either hopelessly incompetent or, more often, he just faded out of the picture. For of course they bored him. All children bored him. So did the overwhelming majority of adults. How could it be otherwise? Their ideas were rudimentary and their reading, non-existent. What had they to offer? Only their sentiments and their moral life, only their occasional wisdom and their frequent and pathetic lack of wisdom. In a word, only their humanity. And humanity was something in which poor Henry was incapable, congenitally, of taking an interest. Between the worlds of quantum theory and epistemology at one end of the spectrum and of sex and pain at the other, there was a kind of limbo peopled only by ghosts. And among the ghosts was about seventy-five per cent of himself. For he was as little aware of his own humanity as of other people's. His ideas and his sensations – yes, he knew all about *those*. But who was the man who had the ideas and felt the sensations? And how was this man related to the things and people around him? How, above all, *ought* he to be related to them? I doubt if it ever occurred to Henry to ask himself such questions. In any case he didn't ask them on this occasion. His soliloquy was not a husband's agonized debate between love and suspicion. That would have been a fully human response to the challenge of a fully human situation – and, as such, it could never occur in the presence of a listener so raw and foolish, so incapable of giving understanding help, as was the young John Rivers of thirty years ago. No, this was essentially a less than human reaction; and one of the elements of its sub-humanity was the fact, the utterly outrageous and senseless fact, that it was taking place in the presence of someone who was neither an intimate friend not a professional counsellor – merely a shocked young bumpkin with a too pious background and a pair of receptive but shuddering ears. Those poor ears! Lucidly expressed and richly documented, the scientific dirt fairly poured into them. Burton and Havelock Ellis, Krafft-Ebing and the incomparable Ploss and Bartels – like Piaget and John Dewey, they were all there in Henry's built-in filing cabinet, accessible in the

54

minutest detail. And in this case, it now became evident, Henry had not been content to remain the armchair expert. He had practised what he preached, he had acted, systematically, on what he knew in theory. How difficult it is, in these days when you can discuss orgasms over the soup and flagellation with the ice cream, how extraordinarily difficult it is to remember the strength of the old taboos, the depth of silence by which they were surrounded! As far as I was concerned, everything that Henry talked about – the techniques of love-making, the anthropology of marriage, the statistics of sexual satisfaction – was a revelation from the abyss. It was the sort of thing that decent people did not mention, did not, I had fondly imagined, even know; the sort of thing that could be discussed and understood only in brothels, at rich men's orgies, in Montmartre and Chinatown and the French Quarter. And yet these horrors were being poured into my ears by the man whom I respected above all others, the man who, for intellect and scientific intuition, surpassed everyone I had ever known. And he was uttering his horrors in connection with the woman whom I loved as Dante had loved Beatrice; as Petrarch worshipped Laura. He was asserting, as though it were the most obvious thing in the world, that Beatrice had almost insatiable appetites, that Laura had broken her marriage vows for the sake of the kind of physical sensations which any hefty brute with a good knowledge of the autonomic nervous system could so easily evoke. And even if he hadn't been accusing Katy of unfaithfulness, I should have been appalled by what he said. For what he said implied that the horrors were as much a part of marriage as of adultery. I can hardly expect you to believe it,' Rivers added with a laugh, 'but it's the truth. Up to that moment I had no idea of what went on between husbands and wives. Or rather I had an idea, but it didn't happen to be correct. My idea was that, outside

55

the underworld, decent people didn't make love except for the sake of having children – once in a lifetime in my parents' case, twice in the Maartenses'. And now here was Henry sitting on the edge of his catafalque and soliloquizing. Soliloquizing with the lucidity of genius, the uninhibited elaboration of infantility, about all the strange and, to me, appallingly immoral things that had happened under its funereal canopy. And Katy, my Katy, had been his accomplice – not his victim, as at first I had tried to believe, but his willing and even enthusiastic accomplice. It was this enthusiasm indeed, that made him suspect her. For if sensuality meant so much to her here, on the domestic catafalque, it must of necessity mean even more to her up there in Chicago, with the young doctor. And suddenly, to my unspeakable embarrassment, Henry covered his face and began to sob.'

There was a silence.

'What did you do?' I asked.

'What *could* I do?' He shrugged his shoulders. 'Nothing, except make a few soothing noises and advise him to go to bed. Tomorrow he'd discover that it had all been a huge mistake. Then, on the pretext of getting him his hot milk, I hurried off to the kitchen. Beulah was in her rocking-chair, reading a small book about the Second Coming. I told her that Dr Maartens wasn't feeling so good. She listened, nodded meaningfully as though she had expected it, then shut her eyes and, in silence, but with moving lips, prayed for a long time. After that she gave a sigh and said, "Empty, swept and garnished." Those were the words that had been given to her. And though it seemed an odd thing to say about a man who had more in his head than any six ordinary intellectuals, the phrase turned out, on second thoughts, to be an exact description of poor old Henry. Empty of God, swept clean of common manhood and garnished, like a Christmas tree, with glittering notions. And seven other devils, worse even than stupidity and sentimentality, had moved in and taken possession. But meanwhile the milk was steaming. I poured it into a thermos and went upstairs. For a moment, as I entered the bedroom, I thought Henry had given me the slip. Then, from behind the catafalque, came a sound of movement. In the recess between the draped chintz of the four-poster and the window, Henry was standing before the open door of a small safe, let into the wall and ordinarily concealed from view by the half-length portrait of Katy in her wedding dress, which covered it. "Here's your milk," I began in a tone of hypocritical cheerfulness. But then I noticed that the thing he had taken out of the recesses of the strong-box was a revolver. My heart missed a beat. I remembered suddenly that there was a midnight train for Chicago. Visions of the day after tomorrow's headlines crowded in on me. FAMOUS SCIENTIST SHOOTS WIFE, SELF. Or NOBEL PRIZE MAN HELD IN DOUBLE SLAYING. Or even MOTHER OF TWO DIES IN FLAMING LOVE NEST. I put down the thermos and, bracing myself to knock him out, if necessary with a left to the jaw, or a short sharp jab in the solar plexus, I walked over to him. "If you don't mind, Dr Maartens," I said respectfully. There was no struggle, hardly so much as a conscious effort on his part to keep the revolver. Five seconds later the thing was safely in my pocket. "I was just looking at it," he said in a small flat voice. And then, after a little pause, he added, "It's a funny thing, when you think of it." And when I asked, "What?" he said, "Death." And that was the full extent of the great man's contribution to the sum of human wisdom. Death was a funny thing when you thought of it. That was why he never thought of it - except on occasions like the present, when suffering had made him feel the need for the self-infliction of more suffering. Murder? Suicide? The ideas had not even occurred to him. All he demanded from the instrument of death was a sensation of negative sensuality - a painful reminder, in the midst of all his other pains, that some day, a long, long time hence, he too would have to die.

' "Can we shut this up again?" I asked. He nodded. On a little table by the bed lay the objects he had taken out of the safe while looking for the revolver. These I now replaced – Katy's jewel box, half a dozen cases containing the gold medals presented to the great man by various learned societies, several manilla envelopes bulging with papers. And finally there were those books – all six volumes of the *Psychology of Sex*, a copy of *Félicia* by Andréa de Nerciat and, published in Brussels, an anonymous work with illustrations, entitled *Miss Floggy's Finishing School*. "Well, that's that," I said in my jolliest bedside manner as I locked the safe door and returned him the key. Picking up the portrait I hung it again on its appointed hook. Behind the white satin and the orange blossom, behind the madonna lilies and a face whose radiance even the ineptitude of a fifth-rate painter could not obscure, who could have divined the presence of that strangely assorted treasure – *Félicia* and the stock certificates, *Miss Floggy* and the golden symbols with which a not very grateful society rewards its men of genius?

'Half an hour later I left him and went to my room – with what a blessed sense of having escaped, of being free at last from an oppressive nightmare! But even in my room there was no security. The first thing I saw, when I switched on the light, was an envelope pinned to my pillow. I opened it and unfolded two sheets of mauve paper. It was a love poem from Ruth. This time yearning rhymed with spurning, Love confessed had caused the beloved to detest her something or other breast. It was too much for one evening: Genius kept pornography in the safe; Beatrice had been to school at Miss Floggy's; childish innocence painted its face, addressed impassioned twaddle to young men and, if I didn't lock my door, would soon be yearning and burning its way out of bad literature into worse reality.

58

'The next morning I overslept and, when I came down to breakfast, the children were already halfway through their cereal. "Your mother isn't coming home, after all," I announced. Timmy was genuinely sorry; but though she uttered appropriate words of regret, the sudden brightening of Ruth's eyes betrayed her; she was delighted. Anger made me cruel. I took her poem out of my pocket and laid it on the tablecloth beside the grapenuts. "It's lousy," I said brutally. Then without looking at her I left the room and went upstairs again to see what had happened to Henry. He had a lecture at nine-thirty and would be late unless I routed him out of bed. But when I knocked at his door, a feeble voice announced that he was ill. I went in. On the catafalque lay what looked already like a dead man. I took his temperature. It was over a hundred and one. What was to be done? I ran downstairs to the kitchen to consult with Beulah. The old woman sighed and shook her head. "You'll see," she said. "He'll *make* her come home." And she told me the story of what had happened, two years before, when Katy went to France to visit her brother's grave in one of the war cemeteries. She had hardly been gone a month when Henry took sick – so sick that they had to send a cable summoning her home. Nine days later, when Katy got back to St Louis, he was all but dead. She entered the sickroom, she laid a hand on his forehead. "I tell you," said Beulah dramatically, "it was just like the raising of Lazarus. Down to the doors of death and then, whoosh! all the way up again, like he was in an elevator. Three days later he was eating fried chicken and talking his head off. And he'll do the same this time. He'll make her come home, even if it means going to death's door to get what he wants." And that,' Rivers added, 'was precisely where he went – to death's door.'

'You mean it was genuine? He wasn't putting on an act?'

59

'As if the second alternative excluded the first! Of course he was putting on an act; but he put it on so successfully that he very nearly died of pneumonia. However, that was something I didn't clearly recognize at the time. In that respect Beulah was a great deal more scientific in her approach than I. I had the exclusive superstition of germs; she believed in psychosomatic medicine. Well, I telephoned the doctor and then went back to the dining-room. The children had finished their breakfast and were gone. I didn't see them again for the best part of two weeks; for when I got home from the laboratory that evening, I found that Beulah had packed them off, on the doctor's advice, to stay with a friendly neighbour. No more poems, no further need to lock my door. It was a great relief. I phoned to Katy on Monday night and again, with the news that we had had to engage a nurse and hire an oxygen tent, on Tuesday. Next day Henry was worse; but so, when I telephoned to Chicago, was poor Mrs Hanbury. "I *can't* leave her," Katy kept repeating in an anguish. "I can't!" To Henry, who had been counting on her return, the news was almost mortal. Within two hours his temperature had risen a whole degree and he was delirious. "It's his life or Mrs Hanbury's," said Beulah, and she went to her room to pray for guidance. In about twenty-five minutes it came. Mrs Hanbury was going to die whatever happened; but Henry would be all right if Katy came home. So she *must* come home. It was the doctor who finally persuaded her. "I don't want to be an alarmist," he said over the phone that evening, "*but* . . ." That did it. "I'll be home by tomorrow night," she said. Henry was going to get his way – but only just in time.

'The doctor left. The nurse settled down to a night of watching. I went to my room. "Katy will be back tomorrow," I said to myself. "Katy will be back tomorrow." But which Katy – mine or Henry's, Beatrice or Miss Floggy's favourite pupil? Would everything, I

60

wondered, be different now? Would it be possible, after the dung-slide, to feel for her as I had felt before? All that night and the next day the questions tormented me. I was still asking them when, at long last, I heard the taxi turning into the driveway. My Katy or his? A horrible foreboding sickened and paralysed me. It was a long time before I could force myself to go and meet her. When at last I opened the front door, the luggage was already on the steps and Katy was paying off the driver. She turned her head. How pale she looked in the light of the porch lamp, how drawn and haggard! But how beautiful! More beautiful than ever – beautiful in a new, heart-rending way, so that I found myself loving her with a passion from which the last traces of impurity had been dissolved by pity and replaced by an ardour of self-sacrifice, a burning desire to help and protect, to lay down life itself in her service. And what about Henry's soliloquy and the other Katy? What about *Miss Floggy* and *Félicia* and the *Studies in the Psychology of Sex*? So far as my suddenly leaping heart was concerned, they had never existed, or at any rate were totally irrelevant.

'As we entered the hall, Beulah came running out of the kitchen. Katy threw her arms round the old woman's neck and for a long half minute the two stood there locked in a silent embrace. Then, drawing back a little, Beulah looked up searchingly into the other's face. And as she looked, the expression of tear-stained rapture gave place to one of deepening anxiety. "But it isn't you," she cried. "It's the ghost of you. You're almost as far gone as he is." Katy tried to laugh it off. She was just a bit tired, that was all. The old woman emphatically shook her head. "It's the virtue," she said. "The virtue's gone out of you. Like it went out of our dear Lord when all those sick people kept grabbing hold of him." "Nonsense," said Katy. But it was quite true. The virtue *had* gone out of her. Three weeks at her mother's bedside had drained her of life. She was empty, a shell animated only by the will. And the will is never enough. The will can't digest your meals for you, or lower your temperature – much less somebody else's temperature. "Wait till tomorrow," Beulah begged, when Katy announced her intention of going up to the sickroom. "Get some sleep. You can't help him now, not in the state you're in." "I helped him last time," Katy retorted. "But last time was different," the old woman insisted. "Last time you had the virtue; you weren't a ghost." "You and your ghosts!" said Katy with a touch of annoyance; and, turning, she started up the stairs. I followed her.

'Under his oxygen tent Henry was asleep or in a stupor. A grey stubble covered his chin and cheeks, and in the emaciated face the nose was enormous, like something in a caricature. Then, as we looked at him, the eyelids opened. Katy bent over the transparent window of the tent and called his name. There was no response, no sign in the pale blue eyes that he knew who she was, or even that he had seen her. "Henry," she repeated, "Henry! It's me. I've come back." The wavering eyes came to a focus and a moment later there was the faintest dawn of recognition – for a few seconds only; then it faded. The eyes drifted away again, the lips began to move; he had fallen back into the world of his delirium. The miracle had miscarried; Lazarus remained unraised. There was a long silence. Then heavily, hopelessly, "I guess I'd better go to bed," Katy said at last.

'And the miracle?' I asked. 'Did she pull it off the next morning?'

'How could she? With no virtue, no life in her, nothing but her will and her anxiety. Which is worse, I wonder – being desperately ill yourself, or watching somebody you love being desperately ill? One has to begin by defining the word "you". I say you're desperately ill. But do I mean *you*? Isn't it, in fact, the new, limited personality created by the fever and the toxins? A personality without intellectual interests, without social obligations, without material concerns. Whereas the loving nurse remains her normal self, with all her memories of past happiness, all her fears for the future, all her worried awareness of a world beyond the four walls of the sickroom. And then there's the question of death. How do you react to the prospect of death? If you're sick enough, you reach a point where, however passionately you may be fighting for life, a part of you wouldn't be at all sorry to die. Anything rather than this misery, this interminably squalid nightmare of finding oneself reduced to a mere lump of suffering matter! "Give me liberty or give me death." But in this case the two are identical. Liberty equals death equals the pursuit of happiness – but only, of course, for the patient, never for the nurse who loves him. She has no right to the luxury of death, to deliverance, through surrender, from her sickroom-prison. Her business is to go on fighting even when it's perfectly obvious that the battle is lost; to go on hoping, even when there are no reasons for anything but despair; to go on praying, even when God has manifestly turned against her, even when she knows for certain that He doesn't exist. She may be sick with grief and foreboding but she must act as though she were cheerful and serenely confident. She may have lost courage; but she must still inspire it. And meanwhile she's working and walking beyond the limits of physical endurance. And there's no respite; she must be constantly there, constantly available, constantly ready to give and give – to go on giving, even when she's completely bankrupt. Yes, bankrupt,' he repeated. 'That's what Katy was. Absolutely bankrupt, but compelled by circumstances and her own will to go on spending. And, to make matters worse, the spending was fruitless. Henry didn't get well; he merely refrained from dying. And meanwhile she was killing herself with the long, sustained effort to keep him alive. The days passed – three days, four days, I can't remember how many. And then came the day I shall never forget. April twenty-third, 1922.'

'Shakespeare's birthday.'

'Mine too.'

'Yours?'

'Not my physical birthday,' Rivers explained. 'That's in October. My spiritual birthday. The day of my emergence from half-baked imbecility into something more nearly resembling the human form. I think,' he added, 'we deserve a little more Scotch.'

He refilled our glasses.

'April the twenty-third,' he repeated. 'What a day of miseries! Henry had had a bad night and was definitely worse. And when, at lunch time, Katy's sister telephoned from Chicago, it was to announce that the end was very close. That evening I had to read a paper before one of the local Scientific Societies. When I got home at eleven, I found only the nurse. Katy, she told me, was in her room, trying to get a little sleep. There was nothing I could do. I went to bed.

'Two hours later I was startled out of unconsciousness by the groping touch of a hand. The room was pitch dark; but my nostrils immediately recognized the aura of womanhood and orris-root surrounding the unseen presence. I sat up. "Mrs Maartens?" (I still called her Mrs Maartens.) The silence was pregnant with tragedy. "Is Dr Maartens worse?" I asked anxiously. There was no immediate answer, only a movement in the darkness, only the creaking of springs as she sat down on the edge of the bed. The fringes of the Spanish shawl she had thrown over her shoulders brushed my face; the field of her fragrance enveloped me. Suddenly and with horror, I found myself remembering Henry's soliloquy. Beatrice had appetites, Laura was a graduate of Miss Floggy's. What blasphemy, what a hideous desecration! I was overcome by shame, and my shame deepened to an intense, remorseful self-loathing when, breaking the long silence Katy told me in a flat expressionless voice that there had been another call from Chicago: her mother was dead. I muttered some kind of condolence. Then the flat voice spoke again. "I've been trying to go to sleep," it said. "But I can't; I'm too tired to sleep." There was a sigh of hopeless weariness, then another silence.

"Have you ever seen anyone die?" the voice went on at last. But my military service hadn't taken me to France, and when my father died, I had been staying at my grandmother's place. At twenty-eight I knew as little of death as of that other great encroachment of the organic upon the verbal, of experience upon our notions and conventions – the act of love. "It's the cut-offness that's so terrible," I heard her saying. "You sit there helplessly, watching the connections being broken, one after the other. The connection with people, the connection with language, the connection with the physical universe. They can't see the light, they can't feel the warmth, they can't breathe the air. And finally the connection with their own body begins to give way. They're left at last hanging by a single thread – and it's fraying, fraying away, minute by minute." The voice broke and, by the muffled sound of the last words, I knew that Katy had covered her face with her hands. "All alone," she whispered, "absolutely alone. " The dying, the living – everyone is alone always. There was a little whimper in the darkness, then a shuddering, convulsive movement, a hardly human cry. She was sobbing. I loved her and she was in anguish. And yet the only thing I could find to say was, "Don't cry." ' Rivers shrugged his shoulders. 'If you don't be-lieve in God or an after-life – which of course as a minister's son I didn't, except in a strictly Pickwickian sense – what else *can* you say in the presence of death? Besides, in this particular case, there was the grotesquely embarrassing fact that I couldn't decide what to call her. Her grief and my compassion had made it impossible to say "Mrs Maartens", but on the other hand "Katy" might seem presumptous, might even sound as though I were trying to exploit her tragedy for the baser purposes of a scroundrel who found it impossible to forget *Miss Floggy* and the dung-slide of Henry's subhuman soliloquy. "Don't cry," I went on whispering, and in lieu of the prohibited endearments, of the Christian name which I dared not pronounce, I laid a timid hand on her shoulder and clumsily patted her. "I'm sorry," she said. And then, brokenly, "I promise I'll behave properly tomorrow." And after another paroxysm of weeping, "I haven't cried like this since before I was married." It was only later that the full significance of that last phrase began to dawn on me. A wife who permitted herself to cry would never have done for poor old Henry. His chronic weakness had compelled her to be unremittingly strong. But even the most stoical fortitude has its limits. That night Katy was at the end of her tether. She had suffered a total defeat – but a defeat for which, in a sense, she was grateful. Circumstances had been too much for her. But, by way of compensation, she had been granted a holiday from responsibility, had been permitted, if only for a few brief minutes, to indulge in the, for her, unprecedented luxury of tears. "Don't cry," I kept repeating. But actually she wanted to cry, she felt the need of crying. Not to mention the fact that she had the best possible reasons for crying. Death was all around her – it had come for her mother; it was coming, inevitably, so it seemed, for her husband; it would be there in a few years for herself, in a few more years for her children. They were all moving towards the same consummation – towards the progressive cutting of the lines of communications, towards the slow, sure attrition of the sustaining threads, towards the final plunge, alone, into the emptiness.

'From somewhere far away over the house-tops a clock struck the three-quarters. The chimes were a man-made insult added gratuitously to a cosmic injury – a symbol of time's incessant passage, a reminder of the inevitable end.

"Don't cry," I implored her, and forgetting everything but my compassion, I moved my hand from the nearer to the further of her shoulders, and drew her closer. Shaken by sobs and trembling, she pressed herself against me. The clock had struck, time was bleeding away and even the living are utterly alone. Our only advantage over the dead woman up there in Chicago, over the dying man at the other end of the house, consisted in the fact that we could be alone in company, could juxtapose our solitudes and pretend that we had fused them into a community. But these, of course, were not the thoughts I was thinking then. Then there was no room in my mind for anything but love and pity and an intensely practical concern for the well-being of this goddess who had suddenly become a weeping child, this adored Beatrice who was now trembling, in just the way that little dogs can tremble, within the circle of my protecting arm. I touched the hands with which she was covering her face; they were stone cold. And the bare feet – cold as ice. "But you're frozen!" I said almost indignantly. And then, thankful that at last it was possible for me to translate my pity into useful action. "You must get under the bed-clothes," I commanded. "At once." I visualized myself tenderly tucking her in, then drawing up a chair and sitting, quietly watchful, like a mother, while she went to sleep. But when I moved to get out of bed, she clung to me, she wouldn't let me go. I tried to disengage myself, I tried to protest. "Mrs Maartens!" But it was like protesting against the clutch of a drowning child; the act was at once inhuman and useless. And meanwhile she was chilled to the bone and trembling – trembling uncontrollably. I did the only thing that was left for me to do. '

'You mean, you got under the covers too?'

'Under the covers,' he repeated, 'with two cold bare arms round my neck and a shuddering, sob-shaken body pressed against my own.'

Rivers drank some whisky and leaning back in his chair,

67

sat for a long time smoking in silence.

'The truth,' he said at last, 'the whole truth and nothing but the truth. All the witnesses take the same oath and testify about the same events. The result, of course, is fifty-seven varieties of fiction. Which of them is nearest the truth? Stendhal or Meredith? Anatole France or D. H. Lawrence? *The fountains of our deepest life shall be confused in Passion's golden purity* or *The Sexual Behaviour of the Human Female*?'

'Do *you* know the answer?' I inquired.

He shook his head.

'Maybe one could take a hint from the geometers. Describe the event in relation to three co-ordinates.' In the air before him Rivers traced with the stem of his pipe two lines at right angles to one another, then from their point of intersection, added a vertical that took his hand above the level of his head. 'Let one of these lines represent Katy, another the John Rivers of thirty years ago, and the third John Rivers as I am today. Now, within this frame of reference, what can we say about the night of April twenty-third, 1922? Not the whole truth, of course. But a good deal more of the truth than can be conveyed in terms of any single fiction. Let's begin with the Katy line.' He drew it again, and for a moment the smoke of his pipe waveringly marked its position in space. 'It's the line,' he said, 'of a born pagan forced by circumstances into a situation with which only a thorough-going Christian or Buddhist could adequately deal. It's the line of a woman who has always been happily at home in the world and who suddenly finds herself standing on the brink of the abyss and invaded, body and mind, by the horrible black emptiness confronting her. Poor thing! She felt herself abandoned, not by God (for she was congenitally incapable of monotheism) but by the gods – all of them, from the little domestic lares and penates to the high Olympians. They had left her and taken everything with them. She had to find her gods again. She had to become a part once more of the natural, and therefore divine, order of things. She had to re-establish her contacts with life – with life at its simplest, life in its most unequivocal manifestations, as physical companionship, as the experience of animal warmth, as strong sensation, as hunger and the satisfaction of hunger. It was a matter of self-preservation. And that isn't the whole story,' Rivers added. 'She was in tears, grieving for the mother who had just died, grieving for the husband who might die tomorrow. There's a certain affinity between the more violent emotions. Anger modulates only too easily into aggressive lust, and sorrow, if you give it a chance, will melt almost imperceptibly, into the most delicious sensuality. After which, of course, He giveth His beloved sleep. In the context of bereavement, love is the equivalent of barbiturates and a trip to Hawaii. Nobody blames the widow or the orphan for resorting to these alleviations. So why condemn them for trying to preserve their life and sanity by the other simpler method?'

'*I'm* not condemning them,' I assured him. 'But other people have other views.'

'And thirty years ago I was one of them.' He ran his pipe up and down the imaginary vertical in front of him. 'The line of the virgin prig of twenty-eight, the line of the ex-Lutheran and ex-mother's boy, the line of the Petrarchian idealist. From *that* position I had no choice but to think of myself as a treacherous adulterer, and of Katy as – what? The words were too hideous to be articulated. Whereas from Katy's goddess-eye viewpoint nothing had happened that was not entirely natural, and anything that was natural was morally good. Looking at the matter from here,' (and he indicated the line of John Rivers-Now) 'I'd say we were both of us half right and therefore wholly wrong – she by being beyond good and evil on the merely Olympian level (and the Olympians, of course, were nothing but a pack of superhuman animals with miraculous powers), and I by not being beyond good and evil at all, but still mired up to the ears in the all too human notions of sin and social

69

convention. To be wholly right, she should have come down to my level and then gone further, on the other side; whereas I should have climbed to her level and, having found it unsatisfactory, pressed forward to join her at the place where one is genuinely beyond good and evil in the sense of being, not a superhuman animal, but a transfigured man or woman. If we had been at that level, should we have done what we then did? It's an unanswerable question. And in actual fact we weren't at that level. She was a goddess who had temporarily broken down and was finding her way home to Olympus by the road of sensuality. I was a divided soul committing a sin all the more enormous for being accompanied by the most ecstatic pleasure. Alternately and even, at moments, simultaneously, I was two people – a novice in love who had had the extraordinary good fortune to find himself in the arms of a woman at once uninhibited and motherly, profoundly tender and profoundly sensual, and a conscience-stricken wretch, ashamed of having succumbed to what he had been taught to regard as his basest passions and shocked, positively outraged (for he was censorious as well as remorseful) by the easy unconcern with which his Beatrice accepted the intrinsic excellence of pleasure, his Laura displayed her proficiency in the arts of love, and displayed it, what was more, in the solemn context of mortality. Mrs Hanbury was dead, Henry was dying. According to all the rules, she should have been in crape and I should have been offering the consolations of philosophy. But in fact, in brute, paradoxical fact . . .' There was a moment of silence. 'Midgets,' he went on pensively as, behind closed lids, he studied his far-off memories. 'Midgets who don't belong to my universe. And they didn't really belong to it even then. That night of the twenty-third of April we were in the Other World, she and I, in the dark, wordless heaven of nakedness and touch and fusion. And what revelations in that heaven, what pentecosts! The visitations of her caresses were like sudden angels, like doves descending.

And how hesitantly, how tardily I responded! With lips that hardly dared, with hands still fearful of blaspheming against my notions, or rather my mother's notions, of what a good woman ought to be, of what, in fact, all good women are – in spite of which (and this was as shocking as it was wonderful) my timid blasphemies against the ideal were rewarded by an answering ecstasy of delight, by a bounty of reciprocated tenderness, beyond anything I could have imagined. But over against that nocturnal Other World stood this world – the world in which the John Rivers of 1922 did his day-time thinking and feeling; the world where this kind of thing was obviously criminal, where a pupil had cheated his master and a wife her husband; the world from whose point of view our dark heaven was the most sordid little hell and the visiting angels nothing but the manifestations of lust in a context of adultery. Lust and adultery,' Rivers repeated with a little laugh. 'How old-fashioned it sounds! Nowadays we prefer to talk of drives, urges, extra-marital intimacies. Is it a good thing? Or a bad thing? Or does it simply not matter one way or another? Fifty years from now Bimbo may know the answer. Meanwhile one can only record the fact that, on the verbal level, morality is simply the systematic use of bad language. *Vile, base, foul* – those are the linguistic foundations of ethics; and those were the words that haunted my conscience as I lay there, hour after hour, watching over Katy's sleep. Sleep – that's also the Other World. Otherer even than the heaven of touch. From love to sleep, from the other to the otherer. It's that otherer otherness which invests the sleeping beloved with a quality almost of sacredness. Helpless sacredness – the thing that people adore in the Christ child; the thing that filled me, then, with such an inexpressible tenderness. And yet it was all vile, base, foul. Those hideous monosyllables! They were like woodpeckers, hammering away at me with their cast-iron beaks. Vile, base, foul . . . But in the silence between two bouts of pecking I could hear Katy quietly breathing; and she was my beloved, asleep and helpless and therefore sacred,

sacred in that Other World where all bad language, even all good language, is entirely irrelevant and beside the point. But that didn't prevent those damned wood-peckers from starting up again with undiminished ferocity.

'And then, against all the conventions of fiction and good style, I must have fallen asleep. For suddenly it was dawn, and the birds were twittering in the suburban gardens, and there was Katy standing beside the bed in the act of throwing her long-fringed shawl over her shoulders. For a fraction of a second I couldn't think why she was there. Then I remembered everything – the visitations in the darkness, the ineffable Other Worlds. But now it was morning, and we were in this world again, and I would have to call her Mrs Maartens. Mrs Maartens, whose mother had just died, whose husband might be dying. Vile, base, foul! How could I ever look her in the face again? But at that moment she turned and looked *me* in the face. I had time to see the beginnings of her old, frank, open smile; then, in an agony of shame and embarrassment, I averted my face. "I'd hoped you wouldn't wake up," she whispered, and bending down, she kissed me, as a grown-up kisses a child, on the forehead. I wanted to tell her that, in spite of everything, I still worshipped her; that my love was as intense as my remorse; that my gratitude for what had happened was as deep and strong as my determination that it should never happen again. But no words came; I was dumb. And so, but for quite another reason, was Katy. If she said nothing about what had happened, it was because she judged that what had happened was the sort of thing it was best not to talk about. "It's after six," was all she said, as she straightened herself up. "I must go and relieve poor Nurse Koppers." Then she turned, opened the door noiselessly and, as noiselessly, closed it behind her. I was left alone, at the mercy of my woodpeckers. Vile, base, foul; foul, base, vile . . . By the time the bell rang for breakfast, my mind was made up. Rather than live a lie, rather than besmirch my ideal, I would go away – forever.

'In the hall, on my way to the dining-room, I ran into Beulah. She was carrying a tray with the eggs and bacon and humming the tune of "All creatures that on earth do dwell"; catching sight of me, she gave me a radiant smile and said, "Praise the Lord!" I had never felt less inclined to praise Him. "We're going to have a miracle," she went on. 'And when I asked her how she knew we were going to have a miracle, she told me that she had just seen Mrs Maartens in the sickroom, and Mrs Maartens was herself again. Not a ghost any more, but her old self. The virtue had come back, and that meant that Dr Maartens would start getting well again. "It's Grace," she said. "I've been praying for it night and day. 'Dear Lord, give Mrs Maartens some of that Grace of yours. Let her have the virtue back, so Dr Maartens can get well.' And now it's happened, it's happened!" And, as though to confirm what she had said, there was a rustling on the stairs behind us. We turned. It was Katy. She was dressed in black. Love and sleep has smoothed her face and the body which yesterday had moved so wearily, at the cost of so much painful effort, was now as softly strong, as rich with life as it had been before her mother's illness. She was a goddess once again – in mourning but uneclipsed, luminous even in her grief and resignation. The goddess came down the stairs, said good morning and asked if Beulah had told me the bad news. For a moment I thought something must have happened to Henry. "You mean Dr Maartens?" I began. She cut me short. The bad news about her mother. And suddenly I realized that, officially, I hadn't yet heard of the melancholy event in Chicago. The blood rushed up into my cheeks and I turned away in horrible confusion. We were acting the lie already – and was I bad at it! Sadly but serenely, the goddess went on talking about that midnight telephone call, about her sister's voice sobbing at the other end of the wire, about the last moments of the long-drawn agony. Beulah sighed noisily, said it was God's will and that she had known it all along, then changed the subject. "What about Dr Maartens?" she asked.

Had they taken his temperature? Katy nodded; they had, and it was definitely lower. "Didn't I tell you so!" the old woman said to me triumphantly. "It's the grace of God, just like I said. The Lord has given her back the virtue." We moved into the dining-room, sat down and began to eat. Heartily, as I remember. And I remember, too, that I found the heartiness rather shocking.' Rivers laughed. 'How hard it is not to be a Manichee! Soul's high, body's low. Death's an affair of the soul, and in that context eggs and bacon are in bad taste and love, of course, is sheer blasphemy. And yet it's sufficiently obvious that eggs and bacon may be the means of grace, that love may be chosen as the instrument of divine intervention.'

'You're talking like Beulah,' I objected.

'Because there aren't any other words to talk with. The uprush from within of something strong and wonderful, something that's manifestly greater than yourself; the things and events which, from being neutral or downright hostile, suddenly, gratuitously, spontaneously come to your rescue – these are facts. They can be observed, they can be experienced. But if you want to talk about them, you discover that the only vocabulary is the theologian's. Grace, Guidance, Inspiration, Providence – the words protest too much, beg all the questions before they're asked. But there are occasions when you can't avoid them. Here was Katy, for example. When she came back from Chicago, the virtue had gone out of her. Gone out of her so completely that she was useless to Henry and a burden to herself. Another woman might have prayed for strength, and the prayer might have been answered – because prayers *do* get answered sometimes. Which is absurd, which is out of the question; and yet it happens. Not, however, to people like Katy. Katy wasn't the praying kind. For her, the supernatural was Nature; the divine was neither spiritual nor specifically human; it was in landscapes and sunshine and animals, it was in flowers, in the sour smell of little babies, in the warmth and softness of snuggling children, it was in kisses, of course, in the nocturnal apocalypses of love, in the more diffuse but no less ineffable bliss of just feeling well. She was a kind of feminine Antaeus – invincible while her feet were on the ground, a goddess so long as she was in contact with the greater goddess within her, the universal Mother without. Three weeks of attendance on a dying woman had broken that contact. Grace came when it was restored, and that happened on the night of April the twenty-third. An hour of love, five or six hours of the deeper otherness of sleep, and the emptiness was filled, the ghost reincarnated. She lived again – yet not she, of course, but the Unknown Quantity lived in her. The Unknown Quantity,' he repeated. 'At one end of the spectrum it's pure spirit, it's the Clear Light of the Void; and at the other end it's instinct, it's health, it's the perfect functioning of an organism that's infallible so long as we don't interfere with it; and somewhere between the two extremes is what St Paul called "Christ" – the divine made human. Spiritual grace, animal grace, human grace – three aspects of the same underlying mystery; ideally, all of us should be open to all of them. In practice most of us either barricade ourselves against every form of grace or, if we open the door, open it to only one of the forms. Which isn't, of course, enough. And yet a third of a loaf is better than no bread. How much better was manifest that morning of April twenty-fourth. Cut off from animal grace, Katy had been an impotent phantom. Restored to it, she was Hera and Demeter and Aphrodite gloriously rolled into one, with Aesculapius and the Grotto of Lourdes thrown in as a bonus – for the miracle was definitely under way. After three days at death's door, Henry had felt the presence of the virtue in her and was responding. Lazarus was in process of being raised.'

'Thanks, at one remove, to you!'

'Thanks, at one remove, to me,' he repeated.

'*Le Cocu Miraculé.* What a subject for a French farce!'

'No better than any other subject. Oedipus, for example, or Lear, or even Jesus or Gandhi – you could make a roaring farce out of any of them. It's just a question of describing your

75

characters from the outside, without sympathy and in violent but unpoetical language. In real life farce exists only for spectators, never for the actors. What *they* participate in is either a tragedy or a complicated and more or less painful psychological drama. So far as I was concerned, the farce of the cuckold's miraculous healing was a long-drawn anguish of divided loyalties, of love in conflict with duty, of temptations resisted and then ignominiously succumbed to, of pleasures guiltily enjoyed and passionately repented, of good resolutions made, forgotten, made again and once more swept away by the torrent of irresistible desire. '

'I thought you'd made up your mind to go away.'

'I had. But that was before I saw her coming down those stairs reincarnated as a goddess. A goddess in mourning. Those emblems of bereavement kept alive the pity, the religious adoration, the sense that my beloved was a spirit who must be worshipped in spirit. But out of the black bodice rose the luminous column of the neck; between the coils of honey-coloured hair the face was transfigured by a kind of unearthly radiance. What's that thing of Blake's?

> *In a wife I would require*
> *What in whores is always found,*
> *The lineaments of satisfied desire.*

'But the lineaments of satisfied desire are also the lineaments of desirability, the lineaments of the promise of future satisfactions. God, how frantically I desired her! And how passionately, from the depths of my remorse, the heights of my idealism, I loathed myself for doing so! When I got back from the lab, I tried to have it out with her. But she put me off. It wasn't the time, it wasn't the place. Beulah might come in, or Nurse Koppers. It would be better in the evening, when we could be quiet. And so, that evening she came to my room. In the darkness, in the perfumed field of her womanhood, I tried to tell her all the things I had been unable to tell her that morning – that I loved her, but we mustn't; that I had never

76

been so happy, nor so utterly miserable; that I would remember what had happened with the most passionate gratitude, all my life long, and that tomorrow I would pack my bags and go and never, never see her again. At that point my voice broke and I found myself sobbing. This time it was Katy's turn to say, "Don't cry," to offer the consolation of a hand on the shoulder, an encircling arm; the outcome, of course, was the same as it had been the night before. The same but more so – with fierier pentecosts, visitations not from mere angels, but from Thrones, Dominations, Powers; and the next morning (when, needless to say, I did not pack my bags), remorses to match the ecstasies, woodpeckers proportionately ferocious.'

'Which Katy, I gather, wasn't pecked by.'

'And resolutely refused to talk about,' Rivers added.

'But *you* must have talked about them.'

'I did my best. But it takes two to make a conversation. Whenever I tried to tell her something of what was going on in my heart and mind, she either changed the subject or else, with a little laugh, with a little indulgent pat on the back of the hand, gently but very decidedly shut me up. Would it have been better, I wonder, if we had come out into the open, courageously called a spade a phallic symbol and handed one another our quivering entrails on a silver platter? Maybe it would. Or maybe it wouldn't. The truth shall make you free; but on the other hand, let sleeping dogs lie and, above all, let lying dogs sleep. One must never forget that the most implacable wars are never the wars about things; they're the wars about the nonsense that eloquent idealists have talked about things – in other words, the religious wars. What's lemonade? Something you make out of lemons. And what's a crusade? Something you make out of crosses – a course of gratuitous violence motivated by an obsession with unanalysed symbols. "What do you read, my lord?" "Words, words, words." And what's in a word? Answer: corpses, millions of corpses. And the moral of *that* is, Keep your trap shut; or if you *must* open it, never take what comes out of it too seriously. Katy kept *our* traps firmly shut. She had the instinctive wisdom that taboos the four-letter words (and *a fortiori* the scientific polysyllables), while tacitly taking for granted the daily and nightly four-letter acts to which they refer. In silence, an act is an act is an act. Verbalized and discussed, it becomes an ethical problem, a *casus belli*, the source of a neurosis. If Katy had talked, where, I ask you, should we have been? In a labyrinth of intercommunicating guilts and anguishes. Some people, of course, enjoy that sort of thing. Others detest it, but feel, remorsefully, that they deserve to suffer. Katy (God bless her!) was neither Methodist nor Masochist. She was a goddess, and the silence of goddesses is genuinely golden. None of your superficial plating. A solid, twenty-four carat silence all the way through. The Olympian's trap is kept shut, not by an act of willed discretion, but because there's really nothing to say. Goddesses are all of one piece. There's no internal conflict in them. Whereas the lives of people like you and me are one long argument. Desires on one side, woodpeckers on the other. Never a moment of real silence. What I needed most at that time was a dose of justificatory good language to counteract the effect of all that vile-base-foul. But Katy wouldn't give it me. Good or bad, language was entirely beside the point. The point, so far as she was concerned, was her experience of the creative otherness of love and sleep. The point was finding herself once again in a state of grace. The point, finally, was her renewed ability to do something for Henry. The proof of the pudding is in the eating, not in the cook book. Pleasure received and given, virtue restored, Lazarus raised from the dead – the eating in this case was self-evidently good. So help yourself to the pudding and don't talk with your mouth full – it's bad manners and it prevents you from appreciating the ambrosial flavour. It was a piece of advice too good for me to be able to take. True, I didn't talk to her; she wouldn't let me. But I went on talking to myself – talking and talking till the ambrosia turned into wormwood or was contaminated by the horrible gamey taste of forbidden pleasure, of sin recognized and knowingly indulged in. And meanwhile the miracle was duly proceeding. Steadily, rapidly, without a single setback, Henry was getting better.'

'Didn't that make you feel happier about things,' I asked. Rivers nodded his head.

'In one way, yes. Because, of course, I realized even then, even in my state of imbecile innocence, that I was indirectly responsible for the miracle. I had betrayed my master; but if I hadn't, my master would probably be dead. Evil had been done; but good, an enormous good, had come of it. It was a kind of justification. On the other hand how horrible it seemed that grace for Katy and life for her husband should be dependent on something so intrinsically low, so utterly vile-base-foul, as bodies and their sexual satisfaction! All my idealism revolted against the notion. And yet it was obviously true.'

'And Henry?' I asked. 'How much did he know or suspect about the origins of the miracle?'

'Nothing,' Rivers answered emphatically. 'No, less than nothing. He was in a mood, as he emerged from the sepulchre, in which suspicion was unthinkable. "Rivers," he said to me one day when he was well enough to have me come and read to him, "I want to talk to you. About Katy," he added after a little pause. My heart stopped beating. This was the moment I had dreaded. "You remember that night just before I got ill?" he went on. "I wasn't in my right mind. I said all kinds of things that I oughtn't to have said, things that weren't true, things, for example, about Katy and that doctor from Johns Hopkins." But the doctor from Johns Hopkins, as he had now discovered, was a cripple. And even if the man hadn't had infantile paralysis as a boy, Katy was utterly incapable of even thinking anything of the kind. And in a voice that trembled with feeling he proceeded to tell me how wonderful Katy was, how unspeakably fortunate he had been to win and hold a wife at once so good, so beautiful, so sensible and yet so sensitive, so strong and faithful and devoted. Without her, he would have gone mad, broken down, fizzled out. And now she had saved his life, and the thought that he had said those wild, bad, senseless things about her tormented him. So would I please forget them or, if I remembered, remember them only as the ravings of a sick man. It was a relief, of course, not to have been found out, and yet, in some ways, this was worse – worse because the display of so much trust, such abysmal ignorance, made me feel ashamed of myself – and not only of myself, of Katy too. We were a pair of cheats, conspiring against a simpleton – a simpleton who, for sentimental reasons which did him nothing but credit, was doing his best to make himself even more innocent than he was by nature.

'That evening I managed to say a little of what was on my mind. At first she tried to stop my mouth with kisses. Then, when I pushed her away, she grew angry and threatened to go back to her room. I had the sacrilegious courage to restrain her by brute force. "You've got to listen," I said as she struggled to free herself. And holding her at arm's length, as one holds a dangerous animal, I poured out my tale of moral anguish. Katy heard me out; then when, it was all over, she laughed. Not sarcastically, not with the intention of wounding me, but from the sunny depths of a goddess's amusement. "*You* can't bear it," she teased. "*You're* too noble to be a party to deception! Can't you ever think of anything but you're own precious self? Think of *me* for a change, think of Henry! A sick genius and the poor woman who's job it's been to keep the sick genius alive and tolerably sane. His huge, crazy intellect against my instincts, his inhuman denial of life against the flow of life in me. It wasn't easy, I've had to fight with every weapon that came to hand. And now here I have to listen to you – talking the most nauseous kind of Sunday School twaddle, daring to tell me – *me!* – you cannot live a lie – like George Washington and the cherry tree. You make me tired. I'm going to sleep." She yawned and, rolling over on her side, turned her back on me – the back,' Rivers added with a little snort of laughter, 'the infinitely eloquent back (if you perused it in the dark, like Braille, with your fingertips), of Aphrodite and Callipyge. And that, my friend, *that* was as near as Katy ever got to an explanation or an apologia. It left me no wiser than I was before. Indeed it left me considerably less wise; for her words prompted me to ask myself a lot of questions, to which she never vouchsafed any answers. Had she implied, for example, that this sort of thing was inevitable – at least in the circumstances of her own marriage? Had it, in actual fact, happened before? And if so, when, how often, with whom?'

'Did you ever find out?' I asked.

Rivers shook his head.

'I never got further than wondering and imagining – my God, how vividly! Which was enough, of course, to make me more miserable than I'd ever been. More miserable, and at the same time more frenziedly amorous. Why is it that, when you suspect a woman you love of having made love to somebody else, you should feel such a heightening of desire? I had loved Katy to the limit. Now I found myself loving her beyond the limit, loving her desperately and insatiably, loving her with a vengeance, if you know what I mean. Katy herself soon noticed it. "You've been looking at me, " she complained two evenings later, "as though you were on a desert island and I were a beef steak. Don't do it. People will notice. Besides, I'm *not* a beef steak, I'm an uncooked human being. And anyhow Henry's almost well again, and the children will be coming home tomorrow. Things will have to go back to what they were before. We've got to be sensible." To be sensible . . . I promised – for tomorrow. Meanwhile – put out the light! – there was this love with a vengeance, this desire which, even in the frenzy of its consummation, retained a quality of despair. The hours passed and in due course it was tomorrow – dawn between the curtains, birds in the garden, the anguish of the final embrace, the reiterated promises that I would be sensible. And how faithfully I kept the promise!

After breakfast I went up to Henry's room and read him Rutherford's article in the latest issue of *Nature*. And when Katy came in from her marketing, I called her "Mrs Maartens" and did my best to look as radiantly serene as she did. Which in my case, of course, was hypocrisy. In hers it was just a manifestation of the Olympian nature. A little before lunch, the children came home, bag and baggage, in a cab. Katy was always the all-seeing mother; but her all-seeingness was tempered generally, by an easy tolerance of childish failings. This time, for some reason, it was different. Perhaps it was the miracle of Henry's recovery that had gone to her head, that had given her not only a sense of power but also a desire to exercise that power in other ways. Perhaps, too, she had been intoxicated by her sudden restoration, after all those nightmare weeks, to a state of animal grace through satisfied desire. Anyhow, whatever the cause may have been, whatever the attenuating circumstances, the fact remained that, on that particular day, Katy was too all-seeing by half. She loved her children and their return filled her with joy; and yet she was under a kind of compulsion, as soon as she saw them, to criticize, to find fault, to throw her maternal weight around. Within two minutes of their arrival she had pounced on Timmy for having dirty ears; within three, she had made Ruth confess that she was constipated; and, within four, had inferred, from the fact that the child didn't want anyone to unpack for her, that she must be hiding some guilty secret. And there – when, at Katy's orders, Beulah had opened the suitcase – there the poor little guilty secret lay revealed: a boxful of cosmetics and the half empty bottle of synthetic violets. At the best of times Katy would have disapproved – but would have disapproved with sympathy, with an understanding chuckle. On this occasion, her disapproval was loud and sarcastic. She had the make-up kit thrown into the garbage can and herself, with an expression of nauseated disgust, poured the perfume into the toilet and pulled the plug. By the time we sat down to our meal, the poetess, red-faced and her eyes still swollen with crying, hated everybody – hated her mother for having humiliated her, hated Beulah for having been such a good prophet, hated poor Mrs Hanbury for being dead and therefore in no further need of Katy's ministrations, hated Henry for being well enough to have permitted this disastrous home-coming, and hated me because I had treated her as a child, had said her love poem was lousy and had shown, still more unforgivably, that I preferred her mother's company to her own.'

'Did she suspect anything?' I asked.

'She probably suspected everything,' Rivers answered.

'But I thought you were being sensible.'

'We were. But Ruth had always been jealous of her mother. And now her mother had hurt her, and at the same time she knew – theoretically, of course, but in terms of the most violent and overblown language – the sort of things that happen when men and women like one another. Ache of purple pulses; lips intertwisted and bitten. Etcetera. Even if nothing had ever happened between Katy and me, she'd have believed that it had, and hated us accordingly, hated us with this new, more implacable kind of hate. In the past her hates had never lasted for more than a day or two. This time it was different. The hatred was unrelenting. For days on end she refused to talk to us, but sat there, through every meal, in a black silence, pregnant with unspoken criticisms and condemnations. Poor little Ruth! Dolores-Salome was, of course, a fiction, but a fiction founded on the solid facts of puberty. In outraging the fiction Katy and I, in our different ways, had outraged something real, something that was a living part of the child's personality. She had come home with her perfume and her make-up, with her brand new breasts and her brand new vocabulary, with Algernon's notions and Oscar's sentiments – had come home full of vaguely wonderful expectations, vaguely horrifying apprehensions; and what had happened to her? The insult of being treated as what, in fact, she still was: an irresponsible child. The outrage

83

of not being taken seriously. The hurt and humiliation of finding herself rejected by the man she had chosen as her victim and Bluebeard, in favour of another woman – and, to make matters worse, the other woman was her own mother. Was it any wonder that all my efforts to laugh or cajole her out of her black mood were unavailing? "Leave her alone," was Katy's advice. "Let her stew in her own juice, until she gets sick of it." But the days passed and Ruth showed no signs of getting sick of it. On the contrary, she seemed to be enjoying the bitter tastes of wounded pride, of jealousy and suspicion. And then, about a week after the children's return, something happened that turned chronic grievance into the acutest, the most ferocious animosity.

'Henry was now well enough to sit up, to walk about his room. A few days more and he would be fully convalescent. "Let him spend a few weeks in the country," the doctor advised. But what with the bad weather in early spring, what with Katy's absence in Chicago, the weekend farmhouse had been closed since Christmas. Before it could be lived in again, it would have to be aired and dusted and provisioned. "Let's go and do the job tomorrow," Katy suggested to me one morning at breakfast. Startlingly, like a prairie dog popping out of its burrow, Ruth emerged from the depths of her malevolent silence. Tomorrow, she muttered angrily, she'd be at school. And *that*, Katy answered, was why tomorrow would be such a good day for doing the necessary chores. No work-shy poetesses mooning around and getting in the way. "But I *must* come," Ruth insisted with a strange kind of muffled violence. "Must?" Katy echoed. "Why *must*?" Ruth looked at her mother for a moment, then dropped her eyes. "Because . . ." she began, thought better of it and broke off. "Because I want to," she concluded lamely. Katy laughed and told her not to be silly. "We'll get off early," she said, turning back to me, "and take a picnic basket." The child turned very pale, tried to eat her toast but couldn't swallow, asked to be excused and, without waiting for an answer, got up and ran out of the room. When I saw her again that afternoon, her face was a mask, blank but somehow menacing, of controlled hostility.'

From outside, in the hall, I had heard the creak of the front door being opened, then the bang of its closing. And now there was the sound of footsteps and low voices. Rivers broke off and looked at his watch.

'Only ten after eleven,' he said, and shook his head. Then, raising his voice, "Molly!" he called. "Is that you?"

Open on a square of smooth white skin, on pearls and the bodice of a scarlet evening gown, a mink coat appeared in the doorway. Above it was a young face that would have been beautiful, if its expression had been less bitterly sullen.

'Was it a nice party?' Rivers asked.

'Stinking,' said the young woman. 'That's why we're home so early. Isn't it, Fred?' she added, turning to a dark-haired young man who had followed her into the room. The young man gave her a look of cold distaste, and turned away. 'Isn't it?' she repeated more loudly, with a note in her voice almost of anguish.

A faint smile appeared on the averted face and there was a shrug of the broad shoulders, but no answer.

Rivers turned to me.

'You've met my little Molly, haven't you?'

'When she was *so* high.'

'And this,' he waved his hand in the direction of the dark young man, 'is my son-in-law, Fred Shaughnessy.'

I said I was pleased to meet him; but the young man didn't even look at me. There was a silence.

Molly drew a jewelled hand across her eyes.

'I've got a splitting headache,' she muttered. 'Guess I'll go to bed.'

She started to walk away; then halted and, with what was evidently an enormous effort, brought herself to say, 'Good night.'

'Good night,' we said in chorus. But she was already gone.

Without a word, as though he were a gunman on her trail, the young man turned and followed her. Rivers sighed profoundly.

'They've got to the point,' he said, 'where sex seems pretty dull unless it's the consummation of a quarrel. And *that*, if you please, is little Bimbo's destiny. Either life as the child of a divorced mother with a succession, until she loses her looks, of lovers or husbands. Or else life as the child of two parents who ought to be divorced but can never separate because they share an unavowable taste for torturing and being tortured. And there's nothing in either eventuality that I can do about it. Whatever happens, the child has got to go through hell. Maybe he'll emerge all the better and stronger for it. Maybe he'll be utterly destroyed. Who knows? Certainly not *these* boys!' He pointed with the stem of his pipe at a long shelf of Freudians and Jungians. 'Psychology-fiction! It makes pleasant reading, it's even rather instructive. But how much does it explain? Everything except the essentials, everything except the two things that finally determine the course of our lives, Predestination and Grace. Look at Molly, for example. She had a mother who knew how to love without wanting to possess. She had a father who at least had sense enough to try to follow his wife's example. She had two sisters who were happy as children and grew up to be successful wives and mothers. There were no quarrels in the household, no chronic tensions, no tragedies or explosions. By all the rules of psychology-fiction, Molly ought to be thoroughly sane and contented. Instead of . . .' He left the sentence unfinished. 'And then there's the other kind of Predestination. Not the inner Pedestination of temperament and character, but the Predestination of events – the kind of Predestination that lay in wait for me and Ruth and Katy. Even through the wrong end of the opera glasses one doesn't like to look at it.'

There was a long silence, which I did not presume to break.

'Well,' he said at last, 'let's get back to Ruth, let's get back to that afternoon of the day before the picnic. I came home from the laboratory, and there was Ruth in the living-room, reading. She didn't look up as I came in, so I put on my breeziest bedside manner and said, "Hullo, kiddums!" She turned and gave me a long, unsmiling, balefully blank look, then went back to her book. This time I tried a literary gambit. "Have you been writing any more poetry?" I asked. "Yes, I have," she said emphatically, and there was a little smile on her face more baleful even than the previous blankness. "May I see it?" To my great surprise, she said yes. The thing wasn't quite finished; but tomorrow without fail. I forgot all about the promise; but the next morning, sure enough, as she was leaving for school, Ruth handed me one of her mauve envelopes. "Here it is," she said. "I hope you'll like it." And giving me another menacing smile, she hurried after Timmy. I was too busy to read the poem immediately, so I slipped the envelope into my pocket and went on with the job of loading the car. Bedding, cutlery, kerosene – I piled the stuff in. Half an hour later we were off. Beulah shouted goodbye from the front steps, Henry waved at us from an upstairs window. Katy waved back and blew a kiss. "I feel like John Gilpin," she said happily as we turned out of the driveway. "*All agog to dash through thick and thin.*" It was one of those lyrical days in early May, one of those positively Shakespearean mornings. There had been rain in the night, and now all the trees were curtseying to a fresh wind; the young leaves glittered like jewels in the sunlight; the great marbly clouds on the horizons were something Michelangelo had dreamed in a moment of ecstatic happiness and superhuman power. And then there were the flowers. Flowers in the suburban gardens, flowers in the woods and fields beyond; and every flower had the conscious beauty of a beloved face, and its fragrance was a secret from the Other World, its petals had the smoothness, under the fingers of my imagination, the silky coolness and resilience of living skin. It goes without saying, of course, that we were still being sensible. But the world was tipsy with its own perfections, crazy with excess of life. We did our work, we ate our picnic lunch, we smoked our cigarettes on deck-chairs in the sun. But the sun was too hot and we decided to finish our nap indoors; and then what anybody could have told us would happen duly happened . . . Happened, as I suddenly discovered between two ecstasies, under the eyes of a three-quarter length portrait of Henry Maartens, commissioned and presented to him by the directors of some big electrical company that had profited by his professional advice, and so monstrous in its photographic realism that it had been relegated to the spare bedroom at the farm. It was one of those portraits that are always looking at you, like Big Brother in Orwell's *1984*. I turned my head, and there it was in its blank cutaway coat, solemnly glaring – the very embodiment of public opinion, the painted symbol and projection of my own guilty conscience. And next to the portrait was a Victorian wardrobe with a looking-glass door that reflected the tree outside the window and, within the room, part of the bed, part of two bodies dappled with sunlight and the moving shadows of oak leaves. "Forgive them, for they know not what they do." But here, what with the portrait and the mirror, there was no possibility of ignorance. And the knowledge of what we had done became even more disquieting when, half an hour later, as I put on my jacket, I heard the crackle of stiff paper in a side pocket, and remembered Ruth's mauve envelope. The poem, this time, was a narrative, in four-line stanzas, a kind of ballad about two adulterers, a faithful wife and her lover, before the bar of God at the Last Judgment. Standing there in the huge, accusing silence, they feel themselves being stripped by invisible hands of all their disguises, garment after garment, until at last they're stark naked. More than stark naked, indeed; for their resurrected bodies are transparent. Lights and liver, bladder and guts, every organ, with its specific excrement – all, all are revoltingly visible. And suddenly they find that they are not alone, but on a stage, under spotlights, in the midst of millions of spectators, tier on tier of them, retching with uncontrollable disgust as they look, or jeering, denouncing, calling for vengeance, howling for the whip and the branding iron. There was a kind of Early Christian malignity about the piece, which was all the more terrifying because Ruth had been brought up completely outside the pale of that hideous kind of fundamentalism. Judgment, hell, eternal punishment – these weren't things she'd been taught to believe in. They were notions she had adopted for her own special purposes, in order to express what she felt about her mother and myself. Jealousy, to begin with; jealousy and rebuffed love, hurt vanity, angry resentment. And the resentment had to be given a respectable motive, the anger transformed into righteous indignation. She suspected the worst of us so that she might be justified in feeling the worst. And she suspected the worst so vehemently that, in next to no time, she wasn't guessing any more, she *knew* that we were guilty. And, knowing it, the child in her was outraged, the woman felt more bitterly, vengefully jealous than before. With a horrible sinking of the heart, a mounting terror in the face of an incalculable future, I read the thing to the end, read it again, then turned to where Katy was sitting before the mirror on the dressing-table, pinning up her hair, smiling at the radiantly smiling image of a goddess, and humming a tune out of "The Marriage of Figaro". *Dove sono i bei momenti Di dolcezza e di piacer?* I had always admired that divine unconcern of hers, that Olympian *je m'en foutisme*. Now, suddenly, it enraged me. She had no right not to be feeling what the reading of Ruth's poem had made me feel. "Do you want to know," I said, "why our little Ruthy has been acting the way she has? Do you want to know what she really thinks of us?" And crossing the room, I handed her the two sheets of purple notepaper on which the child had copied out her poem. Katy started to read. Studying her face I saw the original look of amusement (for Ruth's poetry was a standing joke in the family) give place to an expression of serious, concentrated attention. Then a vertical wrinkle appeared on the forehead between the eyes.

The frown deepened and, as she turned to the second page, she bit her lip. The goddess, after all, was vulnerable . . . I had scored my point; but it was a poor sort of triumph that ended with there being two bewildered rabbits in the trap instead of one. And it was the kind of trap that Katy was totally unequipped to get out of. Most uncomfortable situations she just ignored, just sailed through as though they didn't exist. And in effect, if she went on ignoring them long enough and serenely enough, they stopped existing. The people she had offended forgave her, because she was so beautiful and good-humoured; the people who had worried themselves sick, or made complications for others, succumbed to the contagion of her god-like indifference and momentarily forgot to be neurotic or malignant. And when the technique of being serenely un-aware didn't work, there was her other gambit – the technique of rushing in where angels fear to tread; the technique of being gaily tactless, of making enormous bloomers in all innocence and simplicity, of uttering the most unmentionable truths with the most irresistible of smiles. But this was a case where neither of these methods would work. If she said nothing, Ruth would go on acting as she had acted up till now. And if she rushed in and said everything, God only knew what a disturbed adolescent might do. And meanwhile there was Henry to think of, there was her own future as the sole and, we were all convinced, the utterly indispensable support of a sick genius and his children. Ruth was in the position, and might even now be in the mood, to pull down the whole temple of their lives for the sake of spiting her mother. And there was nothing that a woman who had the temperament of a goddess, without the goddess's omnipotence, could do about it. There was, however, something that *I* could do; and as we discussed our situation – for the first time, remember, since there had been a situation to discuss! – it became more and more clear what that something was. I could do what I had felt I ought to do after that first apocalyptic night – clear out.

'Katy wouldn't hear of it at first, and I had to argue with her all the way home – argue against myself, against my own happiness. In the end she was convinced. It was the only way out of the trap.

'Ruth eyed us, when we got home, like a detective searching for clues. Then she asked me if I had liked her poem. I told her – which was strictly true – that it was the best thing she had ever written. She was pleased, but did her best not to show it. The smile which lit up her face was almost instantly repressed and she asked me, in an intently meaningful way, what I had thought of the poem's subject. I was prepared for the question and answered with an indulgent chuckle. It reminded me, I said, of the sermons my poor dear father used to preach in Lent. Then I looked at my watch, said something about urgent work and left her, as I could see by the expression on her face, discomfited. She had looked forward, I suppose, to a scene in which she would play the coldly implacable judge, while I, the culprit, gave an exhibition of cringing evasion, or broke down and confessed. But, instead, the culprit had laughed and the judge had been treated to an irrelevant joke about clergymen. I had won a skirmish; but the war still raged and could be ended, it was plain enough, only by my retreat.

'Two days later it was Friday and, as happened every Friday, the postman had brought my mother's weekly letter and Beulah, when she set the table for breakfast, had propped it conspicuously (for she was all for mothers) against my coffee cup. I opened, read, looked grave, read again, then lapsed into preoccupied silence. Katy took the cue and asked solicitously if I had had bad news. To which I answered, of course, that it wasn't too good. My mother's health . . . The alibi had been prepared. By that evening it was all settled. Officially, as the head of the laboratory, Henry gave me two weeks' leave of absence. I would take the ten-thirty on Sunday morning and, in the interval, on Saturday, we would all escort the convalescent to the farm and have a farewell picnic.

'There were too many of us for one car; so Katy and the

children went ahead in the family Overland. Henry and Beulah, with most of their luggage, followed in the Maxwell with me. The others had a good start of us; for when we were half a mile from home, Henry discovered, as usual, that he had forgotten some absolutely indispensable book, and we had to drive back and look for it. Ten minutes later we were on our way again. On our way, as it turned out, to that meeting with Predestination.'

Rivers finished his whisky and knocked out his pipe.

'Even through the wrong end of the opera glasses, even in another universe, inhabited by different people . . .' He shook his head. 'There are certain things that are simply inadmissible.' There was a pause. 'Well, let's get it over with,' he said at last. 'About two miles this side of the farm there was a cross-road where you had to turn left. It was in a wood and the leaves were so thick you couldn't see what was coming from either side. When we got there, I slowed down, I honked my horn, I put the car into low and turned. And suddenly, as I rounded the bend, there was the Overland roadster in the ditch, upside down, and near it a big truck with its radiator smashed in. And between the two cars was a young man in blue denims kneeling by a child, who was screaming. Ten or fifteen feet away there were two things that looked like bundles of old clothes, like garbage – garbage with blood on it.'

There was another silence.

'Were they dead?' I finally asked.

'Katy died a few minutes after we came on the scene, and Ruth died in the ambulance on the way to the hospital. Timmy was being reserved for a worse death at Okinawa; he got off with some cuts and a couple of broken ribs. He was sitting at the back, he told us, with Katy driving, and Ruth beside her on the front seat. The two of them had been having an argument, and Ruth was mad about something – he didn't know what, because he wasn't listening; he was thinking of a way of electrifying his clockwork train and anyhow he never

92

paid much attention to what Ruth said when she was mad. If you paid attention to her, it just made things worse. But his mother *had* paid attention. He remembered her saying, "You don't know what you're talking about," and then, "I forbid you to say those things." And then they turned the corner, and they were going too fast and she didn't honk the horn and that huge truck hit them broadside on. So you see,' Rivers concluded, 'it was really both kinds of Predestination. The Predestination of events, and at the same time the Predestination of two temperaments, Ruth's and Katy's – the temperament of an outraged child, who was also a jealous woman; and the temperament of a goddess, cornered by circumstances and suddenly realizing that, objectively, she was only a human being, for whom the Olympian temperament might actually be a handicap. And the discovery was so disturbing that it made her careless, left her incapable of dealing adequately with the events by which she was predestined to be destroyed – and destroyed (but this was for *my* benefit, of course, this was an item in *my* psychological Predestination) with every refinement of physical outrage – an eye put out by a splinter of glass, the nose and lips and chin almost obliterated, rubbed out on the bloody macadam of the road. And there was a crushed right hand and the jagged ends of a broken shin-bone showing through the stocking. It was something I dreamed about almost every night. Katy with her back to me; and she was either on the bed in the farmhouse, or else standing by the window in my room, throwing the shawl over her shoulders. Then she'd turn and look at me, and there was no face, only that expanse of scraped flesh, and I'd wake up screaming. I got to the point where I didn't dare to go to sleep at night.'

Listening to him, I remembered that young John Rivers whom, to my great surprise, I had found at Beirut, in twenty-four, teaching physics at the American University.

'Was that why you looked so horribly ill?' I asked.

He nodded his head.

'Too little sleep and too much memory,' he said. 'I was afraid of going mad, and rather than go mad, I'd decided to kill myself. Then, just in the nick of time, Predestination got to work and came up with the only brand of saving Grace that could do me any good. I met Helen.'

'At the same cocktail party,' I put in, 'where I met her. Do you remember?'

'Sorry, I don't. I don't remember anybody on that occasion except Helen. If you've been saved from drowning, you remember the life-guard, but not the spectators on the pier.'

'No wonder I never had a chance!' I said. 'At the time I used to think, rather bitterly, that it was because women, even the best of them, even the rare extraordinary Helens, prefer good looks to artistic sensibility, prefer brawn with brains (for I was forced to admit that you had some brains!) to brains with that exquisite *je ne sais quoi* which was *my* specialty. Now I see what your irresistible attraction was. You were unhappy.'

He nodded his agreement, and there was a long silence. A clock struck twelve.

'Merry Christmas,' I said and, finished off my whisky, I got up to go. 'You haven't told me what happened to poor old Henry after the accident.'

'Well, he began, of course, by having a relapse. Not a very bad one. He had nothing to gain, this time, by going to death's door. Just a mild affair. Katy's sister came down for the funeral and stayed on to look after him. She was like a caricature of Katy. Fat, florid, loud. Not a goddess disguised as a peasant – a barmaid imagining she was a goddess. She was a widow. Four months later Henry married her. I'd gone to Beirut by that time; so I never witnessed their connubial bliss. But from all accounts it was considerable. But the poor woman couldn't keep her weight down. She died in thirty-five. Henry quickly found himself a young redhead, called Alicia. Alicia wanted to be admired for her thirty-eight inch bust, but still more for her two-hundred inch intellect. "What do you think of Schroedinger?" you'd ask him; but it would be

Alicia who answered. She saw him through to the end.'

'When did you see him last?' I asked.

'Just a few months before he died. Eighty-seven and still amazingly active, still chock-full of what his biographer likes to call "the undiminished blaze of intellectual power." To me he seemed like an overwound clockwork monkey. Clockwork ratiocination; clockwork gestures, clockwork smiles and grimaces. And then there was the conversation. What amazingly realistic tape recordings of the old anecdotes about Planck and Rutherford and J. J. Thompson! Of his celebrated soliloquies about Logical Positivism and Cybernetics! Of reminiscences about those exciting war years when he was working on the A-Bomb! Of his gaily apocalyptic speculations about the bigger and better Infernal Machines of the future! You could have sworn that it was a real human being who was talking. But gradually, as you went on listening, you began to realize that there was nobody at home. The tapes were being reeled off automatically, it was *vox et praeterea nihil* – the voice of Henry Maartens without his presence.'

'But isn't that the thing you were recommending?' I asked. 'Dying every moment.'

'But Henry hadn't died. That's the whole point. He'd merely left the clockwork running and gone somewhere else.'

'Gone where?'

'God knows. Into some kind of infantile burrow in his subconscious, I suppose. Outside, for all to see and hear, was that stupendous clockwork monkey, that undiminished blaze of intellectual power. Inside there lurked the miserable little creature who still needed flattery and reassurance and sex and a womb-substitute – the creature who would have to face the music on Henry's death-bed. *That* was still frantically alive and unprepared, by any preliminary dying, totally unprepared for the decisive moment. Well, the decisive moment is over now and whatever remains of poor old Henry is probably squeaking and gibbering in the streets of Los Alamos, or maybe around the bed of his widow and her new husband. And of course nobody pays any attention, nobody gives a damn. Quite rightly. Let the dead bury their dead. And now you want to go.' He got up, took my arm and walked me out into the hall. 'Drive carefully,' he said as he opened the front door. 'This is a Christian country and it's the Saviour's birthday. Practically everybody you see will be drunk.'